D0784242

LOVE'S OWN DREAM

Roberta Somers was starting a promising new job in the tropical paradise of Jamaica. However, she had a strong feeling of apprehension about her new boss, Justin Martin. Already she had heard that he was engaged to a fantastically beautiful woman, so she knew it was wrong to feel the attraction that was stirring between them. Try as she might to enjoy the attentions of her co-worker, Bill Coffer, Roberta's heart continued to betray her and propel her toward a love that was never meant to be.

Books by Jacqueline Hacsi
in the Linford Romance Library:

PARADISE ISLE

JACQUELINE HACSI

LOVE'S OWN DREAM

Complete and Unabridged

LINFORD
Leicester

First published in the
United States of America

First Linford Edition
published September 1993

British Library CIP Data

Hacsi, Jacqueline
    Love's own dream.—Large print ed.—
    Linford romance library
    I. Title II. Series
    813.54 [F]

    ISBN 0–7089–7454–6

Published by
F. A. Thorpe (Publishing) Ltd.
Anstey, Leicestershire
Set by Words & Graphics Ltd.
Anstey, Leicestershire
Printed and bound in Great Britain by
T. J. Press (Padstow) Ltd., Padstow, Cornwall

This book is printed on acid-free paper

1

AS the elevator doors slid open, Roberta Somers stepped out into the seventh-floor corridor. After checking the directional arrows, she turned to her right and began walking briskly down the hall, trying not to show how tense and nervous she felt, with butterflies doing fancy loops and dive-bombing in her stomach. For the past ten months she'd been employed here in the Los Angeles office of Lovely Lady Cosmetics, working out of the steno pool, but this was the first time she'd ever been on the seventh floor, where the executive offices were.

She reached the door to Suite 703, hesitated momentarily, breathing deeply, then opened the door and stepped inside. She found herself facing a large desk at which no one was seated, but the usual occupant couldn't be far off, Roberta reasoned, as the phone was off the hook, resting sideways on the desk top. A moment later the door to the inner office opened and a pleasant-faced, middle-aged woman stepped through it, closing it behind herself.

"Hello," the woman said with a friendly smile. "I'm Mrs. Andrews. You must be Roberta Somers. Be right with you." Stepping up to the desk, Mrs. Andrews picked up the phone and began talking rapidly into it.

Roberta, shifting her weight, clutched onto her steno pad and long, sharpened pencils a slight bit tighter, nervously glancing around the office, feeling the butterflies inside getting even friskier, dive-bombing from even greater heights.

Mrs. Andrews fell silent, listening now, then a moment later broke in to say, "I'm sorry, Mr. Kendall, but right at the moment I've — " But her caller apparently overrode her and continued talking, for with a sigh Mrs. Andrews sat down, drew a pencil and pad over, and began writing something down, murmuring, "Yes, I've got it, yes, but look — " again apparently being ignored. She slid a palm over the phone receiver, looking across at Roberta. Catching Roberta's eye, she offered an apologetic little shrug before saying into the phone, "Yes, Mr. Kendall, I understand your concern and I assure you — " Again her voice died away.

Two minutes later, after another abortive attempt to terminate the conversation, Mrs. Andrews again slid her palm over the receiver, caught Roberta's eye and said, "Why don't you go on in? Mr. Martin's expecting you and he can explain what the job's all about."

"Thank you, I will," Roberta answered, trying to smile, dismayed to find that her voice didn't work too well; it sounded rather strange, high and thin. Clearing her throat, she stepped forward, taking herself more firmly in hand: head high, shoulders back. How silly to feel nervous just because she was up here, in the rarefied atmosphere! Those who occupied the executive suites were simply people, like everyone else. And she was an expert stenographer who had yet to meet the person whose dictation she couldn't handle!

She opened the door to the inner office, stepped through, pulled it closed. The office was large, half again as large as those on the lower floors, yet not vast enough to be intimidating; and the furnishings — mahogany paneling, dark brown carpeting, a large modern painting with huge red and white splashes — while attractive, were not all that spectacular either. Roberta felt herself begin to relax and a tiny smile played around her mouth. All the energy she had wasted on being nervous! She walked forward toward the desk.

"Mr. Martin?" She spoke easily now, in her normal voice, addressing the man who stood behind the large, cluttered executive desk. "I'm Roberta Somers, from the steno pool, told to report here this morning."

"Oh, yes." He was a tall, broad-shouldered but slender man who appeared to be in his early thirties. He wore glasses, was reading a paper he held, and glanced up so briefly as he spoke that Roberta knew he couldn't possibly really have seen her. "Have a seat, please. I'll be right with you." He continued reading.

Roberta backed up a step and seated herself comfortably in a chair a few feet in front of the desk. She glanced at the man, glanced around the room, took a few casual deep breaths, and felt relaxed and confident. This was only one more man, like the ones she took dictation from every day.

Mr. Martin read another minute or two, then lowered the paper he held, yanked off his glasses, dropping them onto the desk, and pinched his eyes with one hand. The next moment he looked over at Roberta, his eyes narrow as he pinned her under a rude, scrutinizing stare. Roberta felt herself tense instantly again, so violently that she felt a wave of nausea wash through her.

"All right, Miss Somers," the man said, in a clipped, unfriendly voice as he continued to stare rudely at her. "I appreciate your coming here this morning, your willingness to be interviewed. I assume you spoke to Mrs. Andrews in the outer office, is that right?"

Anger stirring within — at the man for staring so rudely at her, at herself for again feeling so nervous and tense — Roberta answered quickly, clear, "Yes, that's right," aware the moment she'd said this that, while the words were true, the impression they would convey was no doubt grossly inaccurate. She tried to gather herself enough together to clarify the situation, but before she had framed the proper words, or any words, Mr. Martin spoke again.

"All right, Miss Somers, I know you're not married," he said, still staring persistently at her, sounding even less friendly. "At least according to the company's personnel records you're not, but nowadays that doesn't seem to mean too much, so let's get it out in the open right now so as not to waste either your time or mine. Even though you're single, I suppose you've got some boyfriend or are living with some man you can't bear to be apart from, is that right?"

Roberta felt a shock wave go through her. She opened her mouth to protest, to snap back, 'Really, I don't see that's any of your business!' but as her eyes met those of her interrogator, she felt a second shock wave, even stronger than the first, strong enough to drown out the first. What a compellingly attractive face she was staring into, framed by wavy black hair, with perfectly proportioned features that seemed chiseled out of polished marble! Why would such a compellingly attractive man care in the slightest whether or not she was married?

"Well, if that's relevant — "

"Obviously it is."

" — the fact is I do live with a man but — "

"I knew it!" Mr. Martin threw himself down on his swivel chair, glaring indignantly at her.

Roberta shifted slightly, pressing backwards, feeling a spurt of triumph as she ended, " — the man happens to be my father."

"*Really?*" Mr. Martin stared a moment longer, then, circling his eyes away, remarked irritably, sneeringly, "And I suppose your father is such a sickly old man you can't possibly leave him?" His dark, piercing eyes circled back and again pinned Roberta down under a rude antagonistic stare.

Roberta stared back, a mixture of emotions — anger, excitement, curiosity — fighting in her. An image of her father flashed through her mind, and 'sickly old man' most emphatically did not describe him. Since her mother's death two years before after a prolonged illness, her father had been keeping steady company with a lively young widow, and, though she still lived with him under the same roof, she rarely saw him nowadays and knew for a certainty that he would not in the least mind having her gone.

"No, Mr. Martin," Roberta snapped coldly, angrily, leaning forward, her pulse pounding furiously, "my father is in no way a sickly old man I can't possibly leave. If it's the least concern of yours, and you seem to be making it your concern, there is no one currently in my life I would have the least objection to being away from."

"Well, good enough! Then would you mind standing, please, and turning around so I can get a better look at you?"

Again taken by surprise, Roberta felt her cheeks instantly begin to burn. After a very slight hesitation she stood up, ready to announce defiantly that she'd do no such thing, she was leaving. But — curiosity held her back. Why in the world was this rude, inquisitive, arrogant man asking her to do this? For what possible reason did he want a 'better look' at her?

As angry as she felt, as ready to announce defiantly that she was leaving, Roberta found herself beginning to turn slowly around, growing hot all over with embarrassment. Thank goodness she'd known about having to come here — she'd been told before leaving work the previous day — and had worn her newest and most attractive pants suit, which was dark blue and fit quite well. But clothes could only do so much; they couldn't do much to round over her thin, awkward boniness into soft, lovely curves. All her life she'd been too tall, and no matter how heartily she ate she couldn't seem to gain weight. Her shoulders were too broad, her breasts too small, her hips too flat, her elbows, wrists, fingers, knees, ankles, feet too bony. It was just one of those things she'd learned to live with, as she'd learned to live with her plain face, but to be put on display like this, to be stared at so fiercely by those rude, dark eyes . . .

As she swung slowly around, Roberta began to feel even angrier, to feel a deep-down fury, while her pulse raced wildly. But surely she was flunking whatever test it was that this crazy arrogant man was putting her through!

"All right, fine," Mr. Martin announced. "Sit down again, please, Miss Somers, if you will. By the way, I'm Justin Martin."

Reseating herself, burning up, Roberta murmured, "How do you do?"

"How do *you* do?" Mr. Martin echoed; then suddenly he smiled, a grin that broke broadly across his dark, chiseled face, causing Roberta to tense instantly even more painfully.

Justin Martin walked around to the front of the desk and sat down on the corner, no longer smiling. "Well, now that you've had a few minutes at least to think about the job — "

Gathering herself together, catching her breath, Roberta broke in, "But I'm afraid I haven't. Mrs. Andrews was on the phone just now; we had no chance to talk. She said you'd explain the job to me."

"She did?" Surprise flashed across his face. "When you said you'd spoken to her, I took it for granted she'd already told you. Well, in that case let me explain what this is all about. We're looking for someone willing and able to take on a three-month assignment that entails leaving this area. All your expenses will be paid, of course; in addition you'll be granted an immediate thirty percent permanent increase in salary, and look at it this way: how often does a young woman like yourself get the chance to travel to a superbly beautiful, exotic country at absolutely no expense to yourself? Surely you'd be a fool to turn down this fantastic opportunity."

Dumbfounded, Roberta tried to take it all in, to gather her wits to frame a coherent answer, but before she could, Justin Martin slid off the desk, slapping his hands against his thighs.

"So if you have no close ties, no one you object to being away from, surely you can be ready to fly to Kingston, Jamaica, by eleven-thirty tonight. As a United States citizen you don't need a passport for a three-month stay so there's no problem there. Meanwhile, I've got business to attend to so I'll leave you now, but you can ask whatever questions you have of Mrs. Andrews, and settle final details with her. I'm delighted to have met you, delighted that you'll be going with me, and I'll see you around ten-thirty tonight."

With a farewell nod in her direction he strode gracefully toward a far door and, yanking it open, disappeared through it.

For several seconds Roberta sat unmoving, still in shock. *Kingston,*

Jamaica? Before midnight tonight? She gave her head a hard shake, then stood up and began walking slowly toward the door through which she'd entered this room — was it really only a few minutes before?

Stepping out into the outer office, she saw that Mrs. Andrews sat at her desk. "Mrs. Andrews," she said, "is that man crazy or what?"

Mrs. Andrews glanced around in surprise, then burst out laughing. "Mr. Martin? Well, yes and no. The fact is he's one of the foremost phytopathologists in the world, that is to say, a plant-disease specialist, and the company has just signed him to a three-month contract to go on special assignment for us. It seems that coconut palms in Jamaica have been hit by a disease that is killing them off, and while the Jamaican government has been doing its best to solve the problem and cure the palms, so far they haven't succeeded.

"For several years now our company

has been working to develop Jamaica as a possible source of copra, which as you know we use in the manufacture of our soaps and cosmetics, so this problem with the palms has been a very real and costly setback for us. Because we have an interest both in bringing the blight under control and also in cementing good relations with the Jamaican government, the company feels it's well worth it to contract with Mr. Martin to go down to study the problem, do you see?"

"Yes, I see," Roberta murmured, frowning. "So he really meant it when he talked about my being ready to fly to Jamaica by midnight tonight?"

Mrs. Andrews nodded emphatically. "Oh, he means it all right, most decidedly. He already has a young assistant lined up who will meet you there in Kingston, but he desperately needs an experienced steno too. For three days he's been interviewing steadily, getting more and more anxious and frustrated. The primary problem is that almost every steno working in this entire building is either married or romantically engaged and consequently turned the assignment down. I spent all day yesterday as well as the day before on the phone contacting private employment agencies trying to engage a male secretary, but without success. This whole thing just came up so suddenly," Mrs. Andrews sighed, "and it's not all that easy to find someone willing to travel thousands of miles away on such short notice."

Mrs. Andrews stood up, walked to a nearby filing cabinet, opened a drawer, and took an envelope out. Walking back, she added, "So I'm sure Mr. Martin is deeply relieved and grateful that you've decided to take the job."

Blushing, Roberta lifted a hand in immediate protest. "Hold on a minute, please. I haven't decided to take it yet. All I'm ready to do at the moment is give it a little thought." Her cheeks beginning to burn again, she murmured in embarrassment, "For one thing, before I'd say yes, I'd want to know why Mr. Martin asked me to turn slowly around in front of him. What made him so interested in what I look like?"

"Oh, I'm sure he wasn't!" Mrs. Andrews protested, but the flush creeping up her cheeks belied her words. "If he asked you to turn around like that, it was surely just to see whether you seem strong and healthy enough. I mean, certainly he would prefer, on an assignment like this, not to engage anyone too delicate or sickly." Mrs. Andrews paused a moment, then faced Roberta and said brightly — a shade too brightly, "Don't you imagine that's it?"

Roberta considered this momentarily, then said, "No, I don't imagine that was it. If he wanted to know whether or not I'm healthy, why didn't he ask me? Besides, he had my personnel record right there and could easily check how often I've called in sick, which I've never once done. And you can tell most about whether people are sickly or not by the way their eyes look, the texture and color of their skin, things like that, not by how a woman is built." Roberta paused, remembering, then added slowly, "So I'm sure he had something more in mind than whether or not I'm healthy and I'd like to know what that something is."

"Oh, I don't think so," Mrs. Andrews insisted, her cheeks still flushed. "Surely not." She paused, biting her lip, then added brightly, "If you mean that he might possibly have wanted to check your looks, well, due to some possible romantic interest, I can assure you that that's not it. The reason the assignment is for three months only is that Mr. Martin refused to sign a longer contract as he is scheduled to marry in three months, and from what he told me and the picture he showed me, the woman he's marrying is very, very beautiful and he seems deeply attached to her. Besides which," Mrs. Andrews added with a nervous little laugh, "he mentioned once that she is not only very beautiful but also quite possessive, so I really don't think Mr. Martin would jeopardize his coming marriage by giving any other woman the eye, if that's what you're concerned about."

"I see," Roberta murmured, her heart plunging down. So that's why she'd passed Justin Martin's test with such flying colors! He hadn't been looking for a female who would interest or excite him, but just the opposite, for one who wouldn't, one who would be sure not to, who wouldn't upset his fiancée or cause any jealous feelings in her. And with me he's certainly gotten the right one, Roberta thought; no woman in her right mind would see me as competition or worry about my being able to steal her man! Sighing, she murmured again, "I see."

"So — you *are* willing to take the assignment, aren't you?" Mrs. Andrews asked anxiously. "I think I can safely say that the company will be so grateful

19

if you do, that upon your return there'll be a nice bonus in it for you. In fact, I give you my word I'll initiate the idea, start the ball rolling myself if no one else does."

"Oh, I'm not hesitating because of the money," Roberta protested quickly, embarrassed now for an entirely different reason. How she could have imagined, for even one moment, that a man like Justin Martin, fantastically attractive and successful, exuding so much power and confidence, had wanted to look her over as a possible, romantic entanglement — how idiotic could one get! Surely she was fully aware of her own limitations by now and knew perfectly well she could never hope to interest a man like that.

"Then why are you hesitating," Mrs. Andrews inquired softly, "if I may ask? Some . . . attachment possibly that you can't bear to leave? If that's it, dear, just say so, and we'll most certainly understand. And it won't affect your job here, believe me. The company recognizes your right not to have your life uprooted between one day and the next at our convenience. But if you don't plan to take the job, the least amount of time we waste discussing it, the better for all concerned. You must see that."

Roberta hesitated for only a split second longer, then plunged in. "But I do plan to take it. In fact, I'm already beginning to feel rather excited about it. My answer is a definite yes."

"Oh, that's great, that's wonderful!" Mrs. Andrews' face broke into a happy, relieved grin. She picked up a paper from the desk and handed it to Roberta, then pressed into her hand the envelope she had taken from the file-cabinet drawer. "So let's not waste any more time; there are a hundred things you'll have to do today, beginning with shopping. Here's three hundred dollars in this envelope to pay for the things Mr. Martin feels you should buy, mostly clothes, which I've jotted down here on this list. For instance, two or three pairs of heavy knee boots, heavy socks — "

Suddenly Mrs. Andrews burst out laughing, backing off. "Well, for heaven's sakes, you can read. I've got it all listed for you. You'll notice that the list is divided between the essential items, mostly clothing, then a few that Mr. Martin considered optional. And please be packed and ready to go by ten-thirty this evening. Mr. Martin will pick you up then to go to the airport. And thank you so much, dear, for agreeing to go. You just don't know what a load this has taken off me! It was getting to the point where I almost felt I'd have to go myself!" Mrs. Andrews laughed again.

"Think nothing of it," Roberta murmured, laughing too. "I'll get right on this list and do my best to be ready on time. Mr. Martin knows where I live?"

Mrs. Andrews picked up a paper, read off an address, and Roberta nodded that that was correct. "He'll know by tonight," Mrs. Andrews assured her, "and while I don't know the man at all well, I have a feeling he's probably a very punctual sort."

"Yes, I imagine," Roberta agreed, remembering the handsome, chiseled face with the dark, piercing eyes, feeling her pulse leap excitedly. "Well, I'd better get going, and — thanks for everything."

"Thank *you*!" Mrs. Andrews exclaimed, and the next moment Roberta was through the door and walking hurriedly down the hall, her cheeks burning, her head spinning, her heart pounding wildly. Tonight, this very night . . .

Before leaving the building, Roberta phoned her father at work to tell him of her plans. His first reaction was, "But if it's for three months that means you'll be gone for Christmas!" which seemed to bother him momentarily; then a moment later he began excitedly discussing the trip with her and soon wished her well. In time, with a sigh, Roberta hung up, one more bridge burned behind her. *Kingston, Jamaica, here I come!* she thought, but it still did not seem in the least real to her.

It began to seem more and more real, however, as the day wore on, especially after she arrived home with her purchases and began to pack. By nine that evening she had her two old suitcases, first used by her parents on their honeymoon trip thirty years before, packed and sitting by the front door, with her small carry-on case half packed and sitting open on her bed.

Shopping had proved to be surprisingly easy and inexpensive; in fact, she had close to a hundred dollars to return to Mr. Martin as soon as she saw him. She had taken the advice jotted down on the sheet and had gone to an army surplus store where she'd been able to buy heavy army fatigue outfits, pants with jackets in olive drab, also sturdy khaki shorts, and a supply of short-sleeved, lightweight T-shirts. She'd also gotten fitted there in tennis shoes and heavy knee boots, buying two pairs of each, and several pairs of heavy socks.

Flashlight, pocket knife, insect repellent — she'd been able to buy them all right there.

After that she'd gone to a women's-wear shop, where she'd bought a couple of sweaters and three bathing suits, one-piece, modest; 'so as not to offend the host population' had been noted on the sheet — but with the kind of figure she had, she most certainly never wore bikinis anyway! Of those items listed as optional she had purchased only one, a battery-operated hair blower-dryer, as her thick long hair tended to take forever to dry and was a bother when it was wet. Apparently — considering the three bathing suits she'd been advised to get — she would be spending quite a bit of time in the water, so the hair blower would come in handy. As for the other optional items — a couple of dresses or pants suits for social wear; a sweater or light jacket for evening wear on social occasions; books, playing cards, jigsaw puzzles, or whatever she enjoyed for leisure hours — she felt she could supply these from what she already had. At the bottom of the list it was noted that Mr. Martin would supply the necessary sleeping bags, blankets, cooking utensils, etc., for overnight camping out, so she needn't give any thought to items of that nature.

Reading that, Roberta had felt her pulse bang hard, excitedly, and she wondered more than ever what she was getting into. She needn't have been warned not to think about buying items of that nature; it would never have occurred to her that, on this assignment, she was going to need a sleeping bag, but apparently she would. As she checked and rechecked her list, trying not to overlook any of the essential items, she did her best not to let her mind wander to that final note; *Mr. Martin would supply the sleeping bags*. The two of them, Justin Martin and herself, camping out at night under a full tropical moon, side by side in their sleeping bags . . .

So just cut that out! Roberta kept ordering herself; *don't think about it*! She did her best not to, concentrating as hard as possible on getting her shopping done and everything safely home and packed; but in spite of herself that image kept sneaking back in: Justin Martin and herself camping together at night in a lovely secluded spot, a huge orange tropical moon over a nearby tree . . .

By nine that night she had everything packed, and at a quarter to ten, bathed, dressed, ready to go, she snapped the living room TV on, sat down in front of it, and tried to get interested to help pass the time. How dreadfully slowly these final minutes were dragging by! Would Justin Martin seem half as attractive to her tonight as he had in the office that morning?

When the ten-thirty program break came, Roberta bounced up to switch the TV off, and she had just done so when the front chime rang. Wouldn't you know it, she thought to herself, right on the dot! With an excited leap of her pulse she hurried to the door to open it.

Justin Martin was just giving the chime bell a second impatient push.

"Hi." Roberta struggled, but unsuccessfully, to hold down the excited grin on her face. "I'm all ready. Won't you come in? My bags are right here."

"Good enough." He stepped in unsmiling, grabbing up the bags, seeming that moment even bigger, more powerfully built, than Roberta had remembered him. In the office that morning he had been wearing a dark brown business suit with a white shirt and tie; but now he wore, Roberta noticed, her pulse racing even more excitedly, a pair of beautifully fitting black corduroy slacks and a black turtleneck sweater, in which he looked, if possible, even more outrageously attractive.

"Here, I'll get the carry-on," Roberta offered, awkwardly trying to reach for it, but Justin, holding one of the cases smashed in under his arm, had already swooped up the small one too.

"No need," he said, in his clipped no-nonsense voice. "If this is it, let's be on our way."

"Right," Roberta agreed, feeling suddenly frightened, out of breath. But in spite of how scared she felt, she switched off the living-room light, plunging the house into darkness, followed her companion through the door, and pulled it closed behind her, which automatically locked it. After taking two steps away up the walk, she stopped and looked back, her eyes suddenly stinging. This small one-story house, its stucco cracking in spots, its yellow paint fading away, was the only home she had ever known. So many childhood and girlhood memories, both joyful and painful, were locked inside it! Yet for the last two years, ever since her mother's death, it had come to seem less and less like a home, more and more just a place where she prepared food once in a while, bathed, and slept.

She didn't really mind leaving it and yet — would she ever be able to come home again? Three months from now, when she returned, would she find it possible at all to pick up the life she had always known and go on as before?

With a light shudder, fighting back her tears, Roberta turned resolutely around and followed Justin Martin up the walk.

Justin opened the trunk of the black car he drove, set her cases inside, said to her over his shoulder, "The door's unlocked, go on and get in," and walked around to the driver's side. Trembling, Roberta opened up the passenger door and climbed in. She was wearing her next-best pants suit, a dark green one, with a pale green sweater under the open jacket; over her arm she carried a light brown coat which she tossed onto the back seat. Settling down, she drew her flat brown purse onto her lap, her fingers nervously clutching it. Flying off into the night, to a strange country thousands of miles away, with an unfriendly arrogant male she couldn't seem to stop thinking about . . .

"Mr. Martin — "

"Call me Justin."

"All right, M — Justin." The name came hard. Frightened, feeling more than a little sick, Roberta began nervously making conversation. "What time exactly does our plane leave, if I may ask?"

"It's scheduled to leave at eleven-forty-five. To Miami, Florida. There's no through flight to Jamaica from here. We arrive in Miami tomorrow morning at seven-thirty, then tomorrow afternoon at two catch a Jamaican plane to Kingston, arriving there at approximately four-fifteen tomorrow afternoon. I don't regret in the least the six- to seven-hour stopover in Miami as that will give me time to locate a laboratory to do our routine testing for us, and get that set up. While I'm doing that, you can do pretty much as you please there, sight-seeing or sleeping or whatever, as long as you're careful not to miss our two-o'clock flight."

By then he'd gotten the car started, had pulled out into the street, and was speeding them off. As his voice died away, he glanced around and offered her a forced little smile.

Smiling tensely in answer, Roberta felt her pulse leap excitedly for the hundredth time that day. Here she was, actually off on this trip, this fantastic adventure, to a part of the world she'd never dared hope to see, with the handsomest man she'd ever met! Surely if she pinched herself she'd wake right up!

"Miss Somers — "

"Oh, call me Roberta, please."

"All right, if you like. All I wanted to mention was how very pleased and grateful I am that you agreed to accept this assignment. In all truth I would greatly have preferred a male secretary as there are bound to be times when we have to put up with very primitive conditions, possibly even sharing the same sleeping quarters if not the same bed, so naturally I would have preferred that it not be a woman.

"Not that you need feel the least concerned in that regard," Justin continued glancing around. "I'm completely trustworthy in such matters and give you my word I won't even think of you as a woman; I'll think of you simply as a fellow employee. So don't give that aspect of it another thought, and as I said a moment ago I am deeply grateful and pleased that you've agreed to come."

"Thank you," Roberta murmured, her pulse calming down. She felt as though a pail of icy water had just been dumped over her head. "I'm very pleased too." Now if only I could stop thinking of you as a man, she thought to herself, for she didn't in the least doubt what he'd said. He simply wouldn't see her as a woman at all, or if he did ever happen to do so it would certainly not be as an attractive or tempting one, certainly not one he'd ever fall in love with; so if she had the least sense she'd stop being so aware of him as an intensely attractive man. He was her employer, period, or, as he put it, a fellow employee. To waste a single moment thinking of him in any other way was simply to invite heartache and hurt.

At the airport Justin took care of everything while Roberta tagged dutifully along, trying desperately not to notice how gracefully he moved, how stunningly attractive he was in his black sweater and slacks, most of all how his very infrequent smiles — he smiled only once, at a young woman who stood in front of them in the seat assignment line — quite literally took her breath away. How could she ever work for him for three whole months and not think of him as a man?

With what seemed astonishing speed they had checked in their luggage, had gotten their seat assignments, and were filing down the ramp onto the plane. Though Roberta had flown twice before, a round-trip vacation to San Francisco, she found it difficult to act as nonchalantly as she felt she should, as blasé as her companion did. Justin politely motioned for her to take the window seat, then he took her coat and carry-on-case and stored them in the compartment overhead. Swinging down onto the seat beside her, he let out a long, satisfied sigh.

"Well, so far so good." He drew the briefcase he'd carried aboard onto his lap, zipped it open, and drew out some pamphlets. "Mrs. Andrews was good enough to gather these together for us, everything that the local office had on hand with regard to copra production and importation. Copra, used in the production of cosmetics, is the dried kernel or meat of the coconut, as I suppose you know?"

"Yes," Roberta murmured, feeling her cheeks flush warmly.

"Well, good enough. Here's a couple for you to check through while I tackle the others." He thrust a couple of sleek, colorful pamphlets at her, his face unsmiling, drew his glasses out, slid them on, and almost at once, frowning, he seemed totally engrossed in what he was reading.

Stifling a sigh, Roberta opened the top pamphlet and began glancing through it. Justin had said she was to check it but she hadn't the least idea what it was she was supposed to check for. Biting her lip, she wondered if she should ask him, decided against it, flipped through several pages, then began reading, beginning with a paragraph that had to do with how coconuts are cracked open with machetes and laid out in the sun for drying.

They'd been in flight for about twenty minutes before Justin spoke to her again. "If you'd get out your notebook, please — "

Startled, Roberta echoed after him, "My notebook — ?"

"Yes, your notebook or your steno pad, whatever you call it, whatever it is you use to take dictation. I'd like to dictate."

In terrible embarrassment, her cheeks burning, Roberta stammered, "Well, I'm afraid — that is, it just didn't occur to me — " But why hadn't it? Because she'd been so busy buying and packing all those items listed, and a steno notebook hadn't been on the list!

Justin bent his head down and eyed her over the rim of his glasses. "You are a stenographer, aren't you? You *do* take dictation?" She would have wanted to sink into the seat if she hadn't, right then, noticed the mere suggestion of a twinkle in his dark, dark eyes.

"Sorry," she said. "I just wasn't thinking, I guess."

Drawing off his glasses, holding them in his hand, Justin grinned at her — and how her insides flip-flopped around as he did! — saying, "Never mind. Doesn't matter. You did such a whale of a job getting ready on such short notice. I'd be a horrible ingrate to cavil over a minor problem like this." He swung out of his seat, began striding away up the aisle, and in less then a minute he was back, handing her a narrow pad of paper.

"Here's an order pad one of the flight attendants was gracious enough to let us have. If you'll just jot down a few things I don't want to risk forgetting, you can type it up for me tomorrow in Miami while I'm off seeing about the lab, all right?"

"Fine," Roberta murmured, drawing a pencil out of her purse and getting poised to begin. It crossed her mind that it was already well after midnight and no one had warned her that she was now on a twenty-four-hour-a-day job, but she'd never before in her life been a clock watcher and she supposed she shouldn't start now. But the fact was it *had* been a long, tiring day and she was edging rather close to exhaustion. If she keeled over in a dead faint, would Justin even notice?

"Okay, first off a note of instructions

to Mrs. Andrews, who's to be our liaison person between the home office and the copra suppliers in the Philippines."

Justin, sliding his glasses back on, began dictating in an extemely rapid, concise fashion that had Roberta's pencil flying over the paper, her heart beating furiously as she struggled to keep up, not to lose a word. After the first fifty minutes of steady dictation — still on the 'note' to Mrs. Andrews! — she ran out of paper and Justin went striding off up the aisle to try to scrounge up another pad. By then it was well past one in the morning after a long, exhausting day, and as Roberta momentarily rested her head back, closing her eyes, it occurred to her that while she very possibly was off on what would prove to be an extremely interesting and exciting adventure, with a 'fellow employee' like Justin, it was most certainly not going to be an easy one.

2

THE pounding on her door seemed to come from a long way off, and she most desperately did not want to hear it. Pressing her head harder into the pillow, Roberta tried to continue sleeping. Then she heard *his* voice and all was lost.

"Roberta, wake up. Long day ahead. Meet you in the main lobby in twenty minutes, all right?"

"Okay." Her voice was a thick jumble of sleep and fatigue."

"Don't fail me. Twenty minutes." Justin's long stride faded away down the hall.

A part of her screamed to rebel, to say the heck with the whole thing and stay right where she was, comfortably asleep in this lovely, warm bed. She was tired. Only two days on her new job and she was already so tired she'd never felt so exhausted in her life. The last thing she needed was to hear Justin's voice calling out that they had a long day ahead. What she wanted for a change was a long night — and a chance to sleep!

On the flight to Miami Justin had dictated for two hours straight, until her eyes had burned with fatigue, her head was spinning, her hand and arm had felt as though they were going to fall off. At last he'd called a halt, suggesting that possibly they should catch a little sleep. 'It'll be a long day ahead in Miami tomorrow, I'm afraid,' he had said. (Whatever had happened to his airy statement in the car driving to the airport such a brief time before that in Miami she would have time to do as she pleased, go sight-seeing or sleep or whatever?) And the moment he'd said this, she had put her head back and had dropped off almost at once, not waking again until the plane began its descent into Miami, which meant that she'd gotten possibly two hours' sleep and who could complain over that, right?

From the airport, once they'd retrieved their luggage, Justin had gotten them a taxi into downtown Miami, where he'd rented a hotel room, one only. 'Which you're to consider yours,' he had assured her. 'After a quick shower and shave I'll be on my way,' which he was. But as much as she'd longed to throw herself down on the bed to sleep some more she couldn't. She had to head out to find a typewriter to rent to type up the endless notes she'd taken on the plane the night before. It was twelve-thirty before she finished that, leaving only enough time to return to the hotel, check out, and catch a cab back to the airport to meet Justin for their two o'clock flight to Kingston. A fat chance she'd had either to see Miami or to rest!

But as the plane lifted in flight that afternoon, Roberta, in a window seat again, sat watching in fascination and that moment it all seemed worthwhile.

The night before, when they'd caught the plane in Los Angeles, she'd had little chance to look down as they were taking off; besides, she'd seen the wide panorama of night lights on her earlier flights; but the aerial view of Miami as the plane rose was truly something: the ocean, the Florida coastline, the narrow strip of Miami Beach, the sparkling blue-green waters of Biscayne Bay. As she sat watching, she realized, with an instantly pounding pulse, that Justin, seated beside her, was leaning over almost to where he was touching her, watching too.

"Marvelous view, isn't it? I imagine you're feeling quite excited by now as I am too. I've only been to Jamaica once before, years ago, and I'm anxious to see how much it has changed. Before three months are up we ought to know the island fairly well."

A moment later he sank back into his own seat, put his glasses on, dove into reading some material he drew out of his briefcase. Work, work, work, that's all he seemed ever to do.

With a sigh Roberta sat staring down at the ocean, then she rested back and stared out at the blue expanse of air, streaked here and there with soft white clouds, and it was all so peaceful and lovely, and she'd had so litle sleep, she found herself dozing off. For over an hour she slipped in and out of a light sleep before Justin, catching her once with her eyes open, asked if she'd gotten his dictation typed up. When she nodded she had, he shot her an appreciative glance.

"Well, good enough. Thank you."

His words sent a delightfully warm feeling spilling through her while at the same time she felt a stirring of annoyance at herself for so thoroughly enjoying his praise. Momentarily, she longed to snap at him that he needn't thank her as she hadn't done it for him; rather she'd done it because that was her job, the reason she was being paid, and all her life she'd striven to give full value in return for her paycheck on any job.

She drew the typed pages out of her carry-on case and sat tensely, all sleep banished, as Justin began checking through them, making occasional corrections by pen — and how that stung, she loathed making mistakes! — but as he finished reading and signed the twenty-page 'note,' he nodded approvingly.

"Very good. Excellent. I can see now why your personnel file had the notation that you are a first-rate stenographer."

As his eyes slid around to catch hers to validate his praise, Roberta felt her heart jump happily. Unable to contain it, she grinned at him, but Justin, to her disappointment, didn't smile back. With a second little nod of approbation, he circled his eyes away, and a moment later began reading more of his endless papers. Sighing, Roberta began staring out the window again, unable, after that, to fall back to sleep.

Two hours out of Miami they were over Jamaica and Roberta got her first glimpse of this tropical island, where the colors — emerald, turquoise, moss — seemed so sharp as to be almost blinding. She stared down in fascination at the lush sparkling blue-green of the Caribbean Sea. Again she was aware as she watched that Justin had lifted up from his seat and was watching over her shoulder, which set her pulse to furious banging. Three whole months . . .

The landing was very smooth; soon they were safely down, once again on land, grabbing up their carry-on bags and lining up in the aisle to disembark.

"Coffer should be here to meet us," Justin commented as they walked across the airstrip, their hair blown by the light tropical breeze.

"Who?"

"Bill Coffer, the young man hired as my assistant. Didn't Mrs. Andrews mention there'd be three of us working here?"

"Oh, yes, as a matter of fact she did," Roberta murmured, just that moment remembering. A regretful sigh rose in her; it wouldn't be just her and Justin after all. Not that it mattered; Justin would never think of her as anything other than a fellow employee anyway!

As they were claiming their luggage, a tall young man with bright red hair and large orange freckles splattered across his face hurried over to meet them.

"Sir, I'm so glad to see you again," the young man exclaimed to Justin, extending a hand, a nervous smile breaking across his freckled face.

"Oh, Coffer, good to see you too," Justin responded, setting a bag down to shake hands. "Roberta, this is Bill Coffer. Bill, Roberta Somers, a first-rate steno who'll be working with us."

As Bill extended his hand, saying, "So pleased to meet you," Roberta offered her own, returning his smile.

"Lend us a hand here, Coffer," Justin said briskly. "We'll check into the hotel; then I've got several things to attend to before dinner so let's get a move on, all right?"

Never a single thought for anything but work, Roberta thought in dismay, grabbing up one of her suitcases as Bill Coffer grabbed up another and they fell into step behind Justin as he strode rapidly out to engage a taxi.

The Jamaican driver, a tall slender black man with gleaming skin and bright friendly eyes, stashed their bags into the trunk, then pulled the doors open, motioning for Bill, Justin, and Roberta to get in.

"The Sheraton-Kingston," Justin said. The driver nodded, climbing quickly in and rolling the taxi forward.

I'm here, I'm actually here, Roberta thought excitedly. This whole trip had come up so fast and she'd been so rushed before leaving Los Angeles that she hadn't had any chance at all to read up on Jamaica, so she knew very little about it. But Justin had mentioned on the plane that the population was about seventy-five percent black or with mixed blood, the descendants of slaves; the rest predominantly white of British descent, East Indian, or Chinese. The official language was English but the mass of black people spoke it in a 'broken' form, seventeenth-century English modified by African speech patterns and dialects. 'When you hear them speaking back and forth among themselves, you'll find you can hardly catch a word of it,' Justin had said.

"Will we be able to stop at least once in the city to have a look around?" Roberta asked now, swinging around to face Justin in the back of the cab. Justin's eyebrows went up.

"This afternoon, you mean? Hardly. Besides, there's little worth seeing in the city anyway, just endless beggars and shills trying to unload stolen or worthless merchandise on you or steal your purse. It's the least attractive part of the entire island and we'll certainly avoid it all we can."

"But — " Roberta protested.

"But what?" Justin countered, scowling at her.

"Well, I — I certainly didn't come all this way without wanting to see as much of the country as I can," she murmured unhappily.

"You'll see it, all right," Justin snapped, swinging his eyes away. "But not today."

Before long they were checking into the Sheraton-Kingston Hotel at Half Way Tree, a modern hotel with four hundred rooms that could, Roberta thought to herself as she looked around her room, have been located just as easily in Miami or Los Angeles. She was still unpacking her suitcases when there was a brisk knock on the door, which made her pulse leap instantly; but it wasn't Justin's voice that called out.

"Roberta, this is Bill. May I come in?"

"Of course, please do." She walked quickly over to open the door.

"Hi," Bill said, stepping in. What

huge orange freckles he had! Overall he was really rather cute, Roberta decided, smiling back at him.

"How you doing?" Bill grinned, running a hand nervously over his bright red hair. "I'm right next door, with Justin on your other side. That's sort of symbolic, don't you think? Woman in the middle and all that. I wonder why they assigned the rooms that way?"

Blushing in spite of her best effort not to, Roberta shrugged, returning to the task of hanging her clothes in the closet. "I wouldn't know, but I can't see that it matters. Are you finished unpacking already?"

"As much as I plan to, but let me warn you from past experience, don't bother unpacking too much. By tomorrow morning you'll have to pack up again."

Roberta, carrying clothes toward the closet, stopped walking. "But I thought Justin said we'd be staying here for the whole three months."

Bill laughed. "Sure we will — for one night out of ten if we're lucky. The other nights we'll be doing well if we get to sleep at all and we sure won't be sleeping in nice comfortable beds like these. I've worked with Mr. Martin before and let me tell you, you don't know what you've let yourself in for. He's a brilliant guy, absolutely totally brilliant, but let me tell you — " Bill shook his head sadly, his grin vanished, his forehead bunched into a scowl, " — he's anything but easy to work for. He's such a super guy himself — smart, strong, tireless — he expects everyone else to be a superman too. I tell you, Roberta, just being in the same city with him, even the same country, makes me feel instantly tense. I felt fine all morning, just great, then as I watched your plane coming down, knowing Mr. Martin was on it — wham, headachy and sick to my stomach, a reaction I just don't seem able to control."

Roberta stood watching Bill's scowling

face. "Then why did you agree to work with him again?" she asked curiously. "I don't understand."

Bill flashed her a boyish, lopsided grin. "Neither do I, believe me. That's what I've asked myself a hundred times this past half hour, ever since I watched your plane coming down. The last time I worked with him I swore that was it, never again, yet here I am. Partly of course it's because I admire the guy so much, he's such a thorough and brilliant worker. And I don't mean he ever gets mean. I've worked with guys who do but Mr. Martin never does. He just cuts you to ribbons with a certain look that says he can't believe how dumb and lousy you are, you've disappointed him so much, and somehow that's worse than being told off, at least for me."

Bill paused, sighing, running his hands nervously over his hair again. "But I guess the main thing is that I thought that this time I'd surely be able to cure my reaction, and one way or another live up to what he wants from me, but I know I won't. I'll disappoint him again and go home with an ego about so big." Bill held his right hand out, pressing his thumb and forefinger together, and the gesture combined with his mournful air made Roberta laugh.

"Oh, come on, Bill, it won't be as bad as all that. I'm sure you'll do fine."

"Sure I will," Bill said. "We haven't even started yet and already I feel bushed, as though what I'd like to do most in the world is dive into bed and sleep straight through the entire three months. Feeling that way, I'm bound to goof up."

"Then stop feeling that way!" Roberta ordered, trying to sound authoritative and stern, while inside she felt both amused and scared. In all truth she felt more than a little sick and tense herself, and had every moment since she'd met Justin; and certainly she felt tired — how inviting that bed looked!

But she also felt extremely hungry and planned to have a tasty, nutritious, leisurely dinner before turning in.

It turned out, though, that while dinner that evening in the hotel dining room was extremely tasty and seemed nutritious enough, it was anything but leisurely. Justin seemed incapable of letting anything be leisurely. After they gave their orders to colorfully dressed waiters garbed in eighteenth-century pirate costumes, Justin plunged immediately into a discussion of what he'd learned that afternoon from his trip to a government office in Kingston.

"I've got a report in my room about the investigation completed so far," Justin explained. "We wired ahead for it days ago and fortunately it was ready and waiting. Once we've finished here" — Roberta's heart sank — "I want to get right on it, condensing it down from the three-hundred-plus pages it is now into workable form for transmission to Los Angeles and our lab in Miami."

The moment their food arrived, Justin dove right into it, as though eating was a tedious task to be gotten through as rapidly as possible, and Roberta felt pressured to eat rapidly too. At one point she caught Bill's eye and he winked unhappily at her, his mouth twitching into a pained little smile. *See what I mean?* his smile said.

After dinner, in Justin's room, the three of them worked together until after one in the morning, sustained by coffee and sandwiches. Having gotten next to no sleep the night before on the plane, Roberta felt so woozy by ten o'clock she could hardly keep writing, but still she managed somehow to take the dictation Justin shot at her and even to get it typed up. When she dared to suggest that possibly she could wait until morning to type her notes, Justin had snapped that no, that wasn't possible, in the morning they'd be getting down to their first real work.

What in the world is this then? Roberta had wondered, typing, gulping down coffee, feeling ready to drop. She remembered what Mrs. Andrews had said about a nice fat bonus upon her return and thought to herself, Well, I sure will have earned it! if only she lived long enough to collect.

Then at a little after one in the morning Justin announced that that was it. "We got a hell of a lot done," he said, "but it's time to quit. Long day ahead of us tomorrow and we need our sleep."

As Roberta weaved uncertainly to her feet, so exhausted she wasn't sure whether she'd be able to make it across the room and down the hall, Justin stepped up beside her and momentarily pressed a hand to the back of her neck, commenting softly, "Your neck's feeling pretty stiff by now, I imagine. Sorry about that, but you've done a really great job and I'm proud of you."

She wanted to think he was praising

more than her work, but realized her foolishness when she saw that even though his voice was soft, his eyes remained as hard and cold as ever.

Drawing quickly away from Justin, throwing him a furious glance, Roberta threw her head back, straightened her shoulders, and found that her anger had given her more than enough energy to walk proudly out of Justin's room and down the hall to her own.

"'Night, now," Bill Coffer said to her at her door, having walked the short distance with her. "Pleasant dreams."

"You too, Bill." Two minutes later she had stripped down, pulled on pajamas, and was crawling into bed, falling immediately to sleep.

But all too soon there was the pounding on the door before she'd had time to get rested at all. Opening one eye Roberta saw it was daylight but still she felt sure she couldn't possibly get out of bed. Squinting at the travel clock sitting on the nightstand, she tried to read it but couldn't; her eyes were too sleepy to register anything. Oh, how she wanted just to put her head back down and fall back to sleep! But Justin expected her to meet him in twenty minutes, so what could she do but throw her poor, tired, exhausted, stupefied body out of bed?

In twenty minutes she had showered, dressed, and was walking across the lobby toward Justin, feeing amazingly awake and refreshed. It was a little past seven in the morning so actually she'd gotten six hours' sleep — did she really need more than that? At the moment she felt that possibly she didn't, for she couldn't believe how alert and alive she felt.

"Good morning," she said brightly to Justin as she reached him, and was instantly rewarded by one of his lovely, infrequent smiles.

"Well, good morning to you, Roberta. You're looking very bright and bushy-tailed this morning. Have you seen Bill?"

"No, I haven't. I knocked on his

door but he didn't answer so I assumed he'd already come down. Did you knock on his door too?"

"You know it," Justin said, laughing, his handsome face glowing. "Well, let's go on to start breakfast without him. He'll surely join us before too long." He took her arm — what a surprisingly warm, gentle touch he had! — and began guiding her toward the dining room.

As Roberta glanced over the menu, she realized that she had never in her life had such a voracious appetite. Every dish listed sounded mouth-wateringly good to her; she felt she could happily order every one.

"Let's both really load up," Justin suggested. "This meal may have to last us till evening, besides which when one is going on less than usual sleep, you can make up for it to a point by eating more."

"You can? I didn't know that."

"Oh, yes. Studies have proved it. So don't be too ladylike; let's both eat like horses." he smiled again.

As the waiter came over, Roberta, feeling impossibly keyed up and energetic, ordered a breakfast fit for a stevedore. "That's the ticket," Justin said approvingly, doing the same himself, and they laughed together.

They were halfway through their huge breakfasts when Bill Coffer, looking extraordinarily thin, lanky, ungroomed and disorganized, rushed up to spill out an apology for being late. "I hate like hell to admit it but I fell back asleep. If you hadn't had the desk ring me up to wake me again, I would probably still be sleeping." The tense, mournful look on his face said he wished he still were, that he felt anything but ready to cope with another long, unnerving day.

"Forget it," Justin said. "Sit down and eat."

Though his words were reasonable enough, Roberta saw the look that flashed through his eyes, the momentary tightening around his mouth, and her heart sank as she could clearly see what Bill had meant the day before. Disappoint this arrogant, demanding man and somehow you felt half an inch tall, your ego felt smashed. Her happy feeling dying completely away, Roberta concentrated on eating, telling herself that she wouldn't, positively *would not* let herself begin to feel as tense and sick as Bill so obviously felt. So what if some time or other — it was bound to happen, sooner or later — *she* couldn't live up to Justin Martin's impossible expectations, so what? She was *not* going to live her life in dread of that moment! Who did the man think he was, anyway?

Breakfast, which had started out so warm and friendly, became another hurried, miserable meal to be gobbled down as quickly as possible in order to get on with important matters.

As they left the dining room, Justin announced they could go back to their rooms, but for fifteen minutes only. He suggested they change clothes, dressing as coolly as possible — shorts, T-shirts, and tennis shoes — and also mentioned that they might possibly want to bring along bathing suits.

"Even at this time of year, early December, it gets very hot here, and quite possibly there'll be a chance to cool off with a swim sometime during the day. Oh, and you'd better bring along a jacket or sweater in case we're late getting back. Better still, throw in a change of clothing or two in case we're really delayed."

"In other words," Bill Coffer muttered out of the side of his mouth as he and Roberta hurried off, "we are off on an extended trip and will be lucky to see our beds again for a week."

"But surely," Roberta protested, smiling, "it won't go on like this very long?"

"Of course not. For three months only, following which you and I will collapse and die and Mr. Justin Superman Martin will take on another assignment and slave-drive some other poor suckers to death."

63

Roberta laughed nervously, though shuddering inwardly, half persuaded of the truth of Bill's words. Maybe taking on this job had been a dreadful mistake after all.

Before the fifteen-minute time limit was up, she was back in the lobby, in the prescribed clothing, carrying her small overnight bag into which she had tossed a swimsuit and towel, a sweater, and two changes of clothing. Although Justin was standing perfectly still, waiting, he gave the impression, as always, of being poised to take off, straining on the leash to get on with it. As Roberta walked up, he glanced at his watch. "I don't suppose you know where Bill is?" he asked impatiently.

Roberta felt her cheeks flush. It could so easily be the other way around, Bill here first and Justin upset with *her* for being half a second late. "No, sorry, I don't. I knocked on his door but he didn't answer so I figured he'd already left. I'm sure he'll be right here."

Justin flashed her a look that said,

'And how can you be sure?' but he didn't say it. "Well, I've got the car all packed and ready to go. Let's go on out and wait for him there." He turned and broked into his usual long rapid stride, Roberta following. Poor Bill, he was sure to get another disgusted look and feel even worse!

They reached a small, dark green car parked in the drive and Justin opened the passenger door for her. "This has been put at our disposal," he said. "I've also arranged for a light plane, but for today, to get more of a feel of the country, I thought we would drive. Obviously one can see more in a car than in a plane." He shot her a quick look, almost smiling.

Climbing into the car, Roberta felt a spurt of delighted surprise. Justin's comment, his decision that they would drive today rather than fly, seemed to be in direct response to her statement the previous afternoon that she wanted to see as much of the country as possible. What a complex man he was, impossible to relax with and yet at the same time impossible to dislike! Her pulse banging wildly, she watched him walk around to climb in behind the wheel and as he did so she smiled at him and he smiled back, which sent her heart soaring. How could she possibly regret having accepted this job?

As Justin's smile faded, he again checked his watch, scowling. Roberta tensed at once again. Oh, why didn't Bill get here? Why must he always be late?

A minute passed, two minutes, five. Roberta kept trying to think of something to say but each time after opening her mouth she would hastily reclose it. Up to now Justin hadn't gotten really angry at her; should she stick her neck out now to side with Bill? Yet — there was no denying that with every passing second she felt sorrier for the freckled redhead, more protective of him. Surely something completely unavoidable was delaying him. Oh, why didn't he get here?

At last they heard pounding steps hurrying up and, glancing around, Roberta saw Bill, red of face, bright orange freckles bouncing, looking taller and thinner than ever in khaki shorts and white T-shirt.

"Sorry, terribly sorry," he panted, yanking the back door open and throwing himself in. Before he'd gotten the door closed Justin had the motor on and the car rolling forward. "I'm dreadfully sorry I kept you waiting but I — I seem to have a bit of indigestion already and — excuse the frankness, Roberta, please — I'm being troubled by diarrhoea, unfortunately."

"No matter," Justin said in his clear, clipped voice. "I'll just drive a bit faster to make up the time. And hopefully your digestion will settle down and stop giving you trouble."

Fat chance of that! Roberta thought indignantly; in the emotional state Bill was in, his physical problems could only get worse. She peered across at Justin, feeling angry at him, and felt her pulse bang again at how handsome he was, even in profile. If only she could learn to dislike him or at least not find him so intensely attractive! If she didn't get herself under better control, she was likely soon to find herself in the same sorry emotional state Bill Coffer was in, except even worse: hopelessly in love with a man she was a nervous wreck being around!

"We're on our way to the north-eastern city of Port Antonio," Justin told them. "With steady driving we should reach there by eleven or so. Obviously it would have been faster to fly, but this way we can relax a bit and get a better feel of the country. Once we reach Port Antonio we'll drive up along the Rio Grande until we're able to rent a raft and take a trip down the river. You'll recall from the report we worked on last night that there are coconut palms along both banks, healthy-appearing trees not fifty feet away from blighted ones, so I feel it's a reasonable place to start. The Jamaican government report indicates, as we noted last night, that the investigation thus far leads to the supposition that the problem is a virus disease, but nothing definitive has been found, which means, in effect, we'll be starting from scratch. Up to now the more I read and study about this, the less I know, the more baffled I am. But with the three of us working on it, somehow we'll crack the case and solve it.

"The thing is, Roberta," Justin continued a moment later, "I work in the field of plant disease, but what I really am is a detective, a latter-day Sherlock Holmes, following one clue after another until I finally have the crucial one that makes all the other clues fall into place. I've heard people refer to me as brilliant, a genius, stupid things like that, but the fact is I'm not. I'm simply hard-working and persistent, and above all I try never to overlook any evidence, for you never know what tiny piece of information will prove to be just the bit of knowledge you need. If I were in fact a genius," he ended, glancing around at Roberta, "I wouldn't have to work so blasted hard, or ask those working with me to work so hard, right? Which is sort of a backhanded apology to both of you for the way I'll no doubt overwork you for the next three months."

"Oh, is that what it is?" Roberta teased, grinning, feeling that moment intensely happy and energetic. "But working hard doesn't mean at all you can't be a genius," she dared to add. "Remember Edison's definition, that genius is only ten percent inspiration and ninety percent perspiration?"

Justin laughed. "Right!" he said. "Except in my case it's more nearly ninety-*nine* percent perspiration and only one tiny percent inspiration. Isn't that right, Bill?" he threw over his shoulder.

"Right enough," Bill muttered mournfully, and as Roberta glanced quickly around at him, he winked sadly at her and shook his head.

By then they were leaving the city of Kingston behind. The well-paved but narrow road they were on was winding into the mountains, with lush green vegetation on every side. As conversation faded away, Roberta turned to stare out at the countryside, at the vivid colors everywhere. Every few minutes they passed people walking along the edge of the road; black women with brightly shining skins and, most often, bright red cotton clothing, knee-length skirts, and blouses; black men in their bright shirts and loose, often cord-tied, trousers. The people walked proudly, heads high, their dark eyes swinging around to eye the small green car as it whizzed past. Repeatedly as the car rounded a curve, another car would suddenly be almost upon them, heading straight toward them down the middle of the road, and, drawing in a frantic breath, Roberta would be sure each time that a head-on crash was inevitable. But each time, Justin quickly steered over to the side, the other driver did too, and the two cars would pass each other with inches to spare.

"Wild, crazy drivers!" Bill exclaimed furiously at one point, after a particularly close brush with another car, but Justin only laughed in response.

"Take one of these Jamaican drivers and drop him onto one of our expressways," Justin suggested mildly, "and he'd think *we* are the truly wild, crazy drivers. Here the roads are narrow and flooding is frequent, so naturally everyone drives down the middle of the paved area until you see another car doing the same thing, then both pull over — "

"Without slowing down by a hair!" Bill threw in.

" — without slowing down," Justin agreed, grinning, "and the moment you pass each other — "

"If you make it!" Bill muttered.

" — you pull back into the center again, as simple as that and thoroughly sane."

"As long as you've got nerves of steel, lightning-fast reflexes, and don't mind flirting with death," Roberta commented softly.

Justin, glancing around in surprise, threw her a broad, appreciative grin which sent delicious shivers down her spine. How handsome he was!

The next moment, feeling a wave of despair, Roberta turned her eyes away and began staring out the window again. To allow herself to keep noticing how darling Justin was, was simply to invite heartache and pain. There was no way she could ever interest or win him, even if he were free, which he wasn't, so she had to stop thinking about him, watching him, dreaming about him! Otherwise she'd never make it through the three months ahead.

She sat staring gloomily out at the landscape whizzing by and before long closed her eyes. The lush tropical growth on each side of the road, with its brilliant colors — green predominantly, but with vivid splashes of flaming red, orange, and purple — began tiring her eyes, and that, along with the smooth forward motion of the little car, made her feel drowsy. Before she realized she was going to, she fell asleep.

Sometime later, as the car rocked to a stop, she woke with a start. Startled, she opened her eyes, confused as to where she was, what was happening. As she glanced around, she saw that Justin was climbing out of the car and she watched him as he strode away.

"Well, so you've waked at last," a male voice said, and glancing around Roberta found herself facing the freckled redhead.

"Yes," she mumbled, feeling anxious and guilty. "How long did I sleep and where in the world are we?" She tried not to say it but couldn't help adding, "Is — is Justin terribly angry with me?"

Bill had the car door open and was poised to climb out. A look of surprise flashed through his eyes. "Angry at you? Heavens, no. He thinks it's great if a person can catch a nap like that. He does it himself every chance he gets. In fact, he kept urging me to nap too; only I'm not like you two, I can't just let go any old where and drop off to sleep. I'd be a hell of a lot better off if only I could." Bill, sighing, climbed out of the car and pulled open the front passenger door for Roberta.

"As for how long you slept, it's close to twelve now, we're on the banks of the Rio Grande, and Justin has gone over there to see about renting us a raft. We're about to go rafting down the river. Doesn't that sound romantic though?" Bill caught her eye and winked, his face breaking into a companionable smile.

Roberta grinned back, laughing softly. Bill was surprisingly attractive, she realized, refreshing in his own boyish way. And she felt he liked her, just as she liked him.

As they began walking away from the car, Roberta saw it was parked in a sizable clearing. To their left the land sloped down very gently to a wide green river. Justin stood over near a dilapidated-looking old wooden house set down among huge flowering trees, talking with three black men near the front porch of the house. She and Bill walked over too, drifting to a stop some ten feet back.

Justin drew out his wallet, handed the tallest of the three Jamaicans two bills, then swung around, walking past Roberta and Bill, motioning for them to follow him.

"Everything's set," he announced, throwing the words over his shoulder as he strode rapidly toward the car. "They say the rafts will only accommodate two passengers and one captain — that is to say, one person to work the pole, which is how they are navigated — so rather than split up and hire two rafts with captains for each, which might prove inconvenient, I told them we'd captain the raft ourselves. So let's grab up our stuff and be on our way."

At the car Justin handed Roberta

a leather case to carry, telling her it contained an expensive, high-speed camera, then he loaded Bill with three wide trays, which had rows of small, empty compartments. He swung up a bulging backpack, strapped it onto his back, then grabbed up the carry-on case Roberta had packed to bring and the smaller case that Bill had brought. After locking the car, he started across the clearing, Roberta and Bill following. They swung down between the trees, striding over the bamboo-stem-strewn ground to the riverbank where one of the Jamaicans had a raft pulled in to shore for them.

The raft, which looked about thirty-five to forty feet long, Roberta guessed, and only three to four feet across, was made of bamboo poles tied together every few feet. Toward the back there was a square platform, also made of bamboo, tied on, and on the back of this platform were two seats, with backrests and cushions. Justin placed their cases on the front of the square platform, took Roberta's arm to help her onto her seat, then motioned for Bill to take the other seat.

"I'll captain us first. I'm sure there's nothing much to it," he said.

After Justin had climbed onto the raft the black man, grinning, handed him a long bamboo pole. Grabbing onto the pole with both hands, holding it crossways, Justin worked his way forward on the long narrow raft. As he got within ten feet of the front, the Jamaican told him that was the right spot for him to be. Justin lowered the bamboo pole into the shallow water, pushed it against the riverbed, and the raft began sliding gently away from the bank. Within minutes they were gliding smoothly down the middle of the river, while Justin pushed with the long pole first on one side, then on the other.

Before long Justin paused long enough to say, "If you look over there, you two, you can see one of the diseased palms. Not fifty feet away there's a seemingly perfectly healthy one, but right there

— do you see it? — there's one that's dying."

Glancing around, shielding her eyes against the bright tropical sun, Roberta squinted in the general direction in which Justin was pointing. Along the river on either side there was thick, green vegetation, but she couldn't see any palms. Lifting her eyes, though, she saw a tree that seemed to be a coconut palm farther back; it rose gracefully, unbranched, high into the sky, then spread out in a crown of leafy canopy. But if there was supposed to be something wrong with the tree, if it was dying . . .

"There's the dead one!" Bill said suddenly, excitedly. "You can tell from the top. Just look! No green leaves, just that burned brown look as though someone had taken a match to it. And not fifty feet away another tree that looks perfectly fine. Isn't that something, though?"

Before long Justin told Bill he wanted him to take over using the pole. As

Roberta sat watching, holding her breath at what seemed to her quite a tricky maneuver, the two men passed each other on the narrow raft, Justin working his way back to where she sat on the little raised platform, Bill edging his way forward, after taking the long pole from Justin, to the proper spot for poling the raft.

Within seconds the switch had been successfully accomplished, and Justin was sitting on the seat beside her, swung around to face the bank, peering out through binoculars at the dying palms.

Since nothing seemed to be expected of her, Roberta tried to rest back and enjoy the ride. She began trailing her fingers in the cool green water and in time decided to take off her tennis shoes and socks and stick her feet in the water too. By then she felt pretty stickily hot and the cool water felt wonderful.

They'd been on the river about twenty minutes when Justin called to

Bill that he wanted to go ashore. Up ahead to the left there seemed to be a break in the thick underbrush where it looked as though they could disembark without much problem and pull the raft onto the bank.

"Up there, Bill," Justin pointed out. "Pull us in there."

"Right, sir," Bill called back. "I'll do my best anyway." He began using the pole on one side only, trying to maneuver them in.

As they began edging their way unevenly toward shore, they encountered an area where huge rocks were barely covered by the river water, and a row of rocks jutting up above water level created a miniature rapids. Bill, struggling with the pole, trying to take them in to shore, hit a rock with his pole, pushed too hard, and the next thing Roberta knew she could feel the raft under her heaving up, overturning.

"Oh my God!" she heard Justin exclaim, almost at the same time she heard Bill yell out, "Oh, Lord, watch it!" All Roberta could think of, as she felt her self plunging into the water, was that the leather case she held, suspended from straps around her neck, contained, according to Justin, an expensive camera. Grabbing it up with both hands, she struggled to keep it aloft, out of the water as she felt herself sinking down, her legs, hips, and back scraping against jutting rocks.

Within moments she was able to wiggle her way back up, to where her head was above the water. Holding the camera up, with effort she struggled toward the riverbank, where she faced a huge overhanging rock surrounded by thick, rough underbrush. Panting for breath, coughing water up, she tried to locate a rock to stand on, for the water here seemed over her head, but she couldn't find one. In time, still more worried about the camera than anything else, she began clutching onto underbrush with one hand to hold herself up while holding the camera above water with the other.

Only then did she have the chance to see how her companions were faring. The raft was already some seventy to eighty feet farther downstream, upside down. Bill was running down a strip of sand mid-river, apparently hoping to catch up with the raft, while Justin . . .

Suddenly Roberta grinned. Wouldn't you know it? Justin, in the water, had already caught up with the raft, was holding it on one side, pushing it toward the strip of land down which Bill was running.

As Roberta watched, Bill waded out and the two men pulled the raft onto the sand. They managed to right it, Justin went for the pole, which had beached itself some twenty feet back; then the two men stood talking and gesturing and Roberta knew they were discussing how best to come back to rescue her, as well as the two cases, hers and Bill's, which were bobbing along in the river.

"Just hold on!" Justin yelled at her,

his clipped voice carrying clearly in the hot, still air. "We'll be right there."

"Right," Roberta yelled back, wondering what her alternatives were. She was in water up to her chest, her right arm, holding the camera aloft, was beginning to ache like the devil; her left arm was scratched and bleeding from the underbrush she was clinging onto; her legs, hips, and back were bruised and hurting from her fall onto the rocks; on top of that she felt suddenly terribly hungry and nauseated.

If my friends back home could only see me now! she thought wryly, gritting her teeth against the pain, not sure whether she wanted to laugh or cry.

3

BILL COFFER had mournfully predicted that they wouldn't see a bed again for a week. This turned out to be a gross under-estimation; apart from one mad dash back to the hotel to pick up additional clothing and equipment, they did not sleep in regular beds again for three times that long.

For three weeks they worked along the riverbank, rarely wandering more than two or three hundred yards from the spot where the raft had overturned. After surveying the area, Justin chose one obviously blighted palm, another apparently healthy one close by, and said that to begin with they would concentrate on studying these two trees, then would match up ten or twelve others.

"You see, ordinarily," he explained

to Roberta, "if you find healthy trees growing side by side with unhealthy ones, you can immediately eliminate physiogenic factors — that is to say, nonparasitic factors — as a cause of the disease. By physiogenic factors I mean possible toxic chemicals in the environment, possible nutrient deprivation in the soil or water, undetected starvation, things of that sort. By all rights we should be able to write that off immediately, shouldn't we?"

Justin stood by her side, staring up at the blighted tree he had chosen for examination, and as Roberta, shielding her eyes with her hand, stared up at the tree too, she felt instinctively that she was being led into a verbal trap. If she agreed that yes, certainly they should be able to write off physiogenic factors, Justin would immediately leap in and pounce on her error in reasoning, showing her how grievously wrong she was. Yet if she argued with him, disagreeing with his statement — oh, heavens, she hadn't the least idea really, and did it matter that she didn't? She was only here as a stenographer, knew nothing at all about trees or their diseases, and in all truth cared even less.

When she didn't answer at once, just stood by Justin's side staring absently up at the dying palm, annoyed with him for posing the riddle to her, she became aware that Justin's eyes had lowered and that he was now fixing her with his insistent, inquisitive stare.

With a slight blush, she dropped her own eyes and turned to face him.

"The truth is, you just don't give a hang about it, do you?" Justin asked, his voice surprisingly soft, his eyes . . . Could that possibly be a hint of disappointment flashing way down deep inside them?

Roberta could feel her face flush even more warmly. She opened her mouth to protest, to lie, and then, with an embarrassed little smile, confessed, "No, I guess not. Should I? I mean — "

"You mean," Justin supplied as her voice died away, "you're not here to think, you're not being paid to think. Just do your job and let me worry about the why and wherefore of what I ask you to do. Well, if that's how you want it . . . "

As his voice faded, they stood for a time looking steadily at each other, Roberta's pulse beginning to pound at the frightening intimacy of the exchange. This was the first time Justin had tried to offer her some understanding of the work they would be doing, so why was she resisting?

"I'm sorry," Roberta murmured after another moment, at last able to pull her eyes free of Justin's. "I really would like to hear whatever you were going to tell me, so ask the question again, would you please?"

To her surprise, Justin remained silent. Roberta in time, her pulse leaping furiously again, glanced back to face him, puzzled. She caught him eyeing her steadily, his eyes gleaming.

"Surely a keen curiosity about the world we live in is a healthy thing, isn't it?" he challenged her. "You should want to hear what I have to say not because we're both here about to dive into strenuous work, not because we happen to be fellow employees sharing the same assignment, not because it might make the work seem a little less tedious and arduous if you understand why we're doing it, but for the pure intellectual pleasure and excitement of adding to your understanding of this marvelous world we live in, don't you think so?"

After meeting his glance for a moment, Roberta burst out laughing. "You're right, of course. But I've already apologized once for the disinterest I showed. Isn't once enough? Can't we forget it and proceed?"

"Right," Justin murmured, and as Roberta laughed again, he grinned broadly, then laughed too. "If you're sure you're ready now to listen — "

"I'm sure, I'm sure."

"All right, as I was saying, when you have a situation like this, with healthy trees growing right alongside ones that are obviously diseased, you can ordinarily assume you are dealing with a pathogenic disease, that is, a disease caused by infectious agents. Surely you can see the reasoning behind that?"

"Well — " Roberta again shielded her eyes to stare up at the diseased palm. "I — I — " It was so hot; she was tired. Above all, Justin's presence, his unsettling nearness, so unnerved her it was terribly hard to think; besides which, she suddenly realized, it had been quite a time since she had really tried to think. When had she last challenged her mind in any way, tried to reason anything out? Physiogenic causes versus pathogenic causes . . .

"Well, it — it's so awfully hot," Roberta murmured finally in answer, dropping her eyes again, and again facing Justin. Couldn't he please help her out? her eyes asked.

"Roberta, it's really extraordinarily simple," Justin remarked patiently, like a dedicated teacher doing his best to lead a reluctant student to knowledge. "Environmental factors seldom vary drastically over a small area, so that if it were nonliving factors blighting this tree, then every tree in the area would be similarly blighted. For instance, if the soil here lacks some nutrient vital to the life of these palms, if that's why this palm here is dying, then that palm over there, thirty feet away, would be dying too. That's why we can ordinarily rule out nonliving factors in a situation of this kind."

"Only — this time we can't?" Roberta ventured after a moment, still so unsettled by Justin's nearness, by his eyes continually turning to look into hers, that trying to think at all was like trying to run through sand.

"That's right, only this time we can't. Can you guess why?"

Again Roberta shielded her eyes to frown up at the palm. After a long moment, dropping her eyes again, she faced Justin, grinning. "Haven't the foggiest," she said. "Why can't we?"

"Because," Justin said, with an answering grin, "the pattern of blighting among the palms here has been so erratic, so without apparent rhyme or reason, that neither you nor I has the least certainty that every tree in the area isn't similarly blighted without yet showing the outward symptoms. In other words, every coconut palm on the entire island of Jamaica may be well on the way to dying already — just as people can carry hidden cancers around for some time and not know it — dying from some unknown environmental factor not yet detected. So, unfortunately," Justin ended with a sigh, "we can't rule out anything, we must start from absolute scratch."

As Justin fell silent, his grin vanished; Roberta felt her pulse almost burst. To be here with him, miles away from everything, to know that they would be working together, side by side, for three whole months . . .

"So shall we get at it?" Justin asked. "We've no time to lose."

"Right!" Roberta agreed, smiling, feeling suddenly energized to do whatever Justin told her to do.

Bill returned within minutes and Justin set them to work measuring and digging. He wanted soil samples from around each of the two trees, both the healthy one he had chosen and the blighted one, at prescribed distances from the base. The soil samples were to come from varying depths: surface soil, two inches down, six inches down, one foot down, three feet down five feet down, each sample carefully labeled as it was put in the specimen tray. For today they would gather only to the six-inch level, with the small folding shovel they had.

"As soon as these trays are full, we'll drive down to Port Antonio and mail the samples to our lab in Miami," Justin explained, "where they'll be analyzed and compared to similar samples that will be flown in from the Philippines. That's how good detectives work. So let's get on it, all right?"

"Righto," Bill Coffer muttered, gathering the equipment they needed — specimen trays, tape measure, spoon, labels — glancing mournfully at Roberta in a way that caused her to burst into happy laughter. How excited and keyed up she felt! Would she never get used to being around Justin?

While she and Bill got to work, Justin disappeared for a time. The next time Roberta, glancing around, was able to locate him her heart almost stopped: he was fifty feet up a palm, climbing even higher. In spite of herself, Roberta stopped working, shielding her eyes against the hot sun as she watched Justin skim rapidly up the smooth palm trunk.

"Just look at him go!" she murmured admiringly to Bill, awed by the sight.

Bill stopped working and glanced up too. "He's good all right," Bill admitted grudgingly, "but you should see the natives here climb. No equipment of any kind, barefooted, just stick a knife in their belts and up they go. I'm surprised superman Martin doesn't give that a try!"

His voice sounded so thin and querulous that Roberta, unpleasantly struck by it, dropped her gaze to meet Bill's eyes. "You really don't like him, do you?" she said in surprise.

Bill's eyes met hers, then a light flush crept over his freckled face. Grinning sheepishly he said, "Of course I like him — can't you detect terrible envy when you hear it? I only wish I were half the man he is." With a deep sigh and a sad little shake of his head, Bill returned his attention to the work at hand, spooning up a specimen of soil, and Roberta, sighing also, did too.

The time sped by with amazing swiftness and before she expected it Justin walked over to mention it was almost six o'clock, was she hungry yet? Startled by his question, Roberta glanced up, trying to toss her head to push back an annoying strand of hair that had fallen down over her eyes; her hands were so dirt encrusted she didn't want to use them to do it. Noticing, Justin reached down and lifted up the strand for her, carefully placing it back where it belonged. As something in Roberta tensed instantly with pleasure, Justin smiled at her.

"You've really been slaving away," Justin commented appreciatively. "Where's Bill?"

"Oh, you know," Roberta answered with some embarrassment, motioning with her shoulder toward a clump of bamboo trees in the middle of which Bill had set up the portable toilet brought from the car. "I'm sure he'll be right back."

"Poor guy," Justin murmured. "So what about you — ready to knock off yet for the day?"

"All right, in a minute. As soon as I finish this one last dig."

Justin straightened up again — he had bent down to talk to her near where she crouched — and after a momentary hesitation said, "Good enough," and turned away.

Within a few minutes Roberta had finished, Bill returned, and Justin suggested they all bathe in the river, then go back to the car and drive down to Port Antonio for dinner.

"A luxury we won't often afford ourselves," Justin explained, smiling, "but we've put in a good day's work and deserve it today. Besides, there are several things I want to buy so we might as well make the trip today."

"Otherwise we'd postpone it indefinitely," Bill muttered as an aside to Roberta which caused her to laugh as she shot him a quick, exasperated look. She herself, suddenly aware that she felt very hungry, was delighted to hear they were going to go into town to eat; why couldn't Bill ever enjoy such lovely treats instead of always knocking everything?

Quickly changing into her bathing suit, Roberta plunged into the river to wash off — and how marvelous the water felt! Although it was early evening already, it was still humid and warm. How refreshingly the water cleansed and cooled her! After soaping herself with a bar that Justin, grinning, tossed to her, she lay on her back in the shallow river, feeling her hair float out all around her head, her aching limbs relax, her whole body give itself up to the overpowering intoxication of the moment. How fantastically happy she felt, and so alive and strong! Never before in her life could she remember feeling quite as content, quite as completely at peace with herself. To be here like this, doing important work, accompanied by two interesting and attractive men . . . With a smile Roberta closed her eyes and floated happily on her back.

She got through the evening in fine style, the raft trip — poling against the current — back to where their car was, walking to the car, the drive into town, dinner in a small restaurant catering to tourists, walking around town for an hour with Bill while Justin went off to scrounge up the supplies he wanted, then the drive back, the decision to sleep in and around the car for the night . . . As far as Roberta could remember the next day, the very moment she'd climbed into her sleeping bag she was out, gone, fast asleep. She couldn't even remember saying good-night to either Justin or Bill.

Sunlight on her face woke her, or possibly it was the sound of leaves crunching underfoot as Justin walked to and from the car, loading things onto the raft. Startled awake, blinking, momentarily confused as to where she was, Roberta turned over onto her side and stared out at her surroundings: trees, a bamboo-strewn ground, off in the distance a dilapidated old wooden house. Then she knew exactly where she was, and how happy she'd felt climbing into her sleeping bag the night before, how happy she felt now!

With a grin she reached up, stretching, then unzipped her bag and climbed out — or tried to.

Wow! Trying to stand up, she found she could hardly move. Talk about stiff — she had never felt so painfully stiff in all her life. With great effort she managed to stand, but as she tried to move further, to take a step . . . Oh, she couldn't; every muscle in her whole body screamed, from her toes to her shoulders — every single muscle, many of which she had never even known before that she had. If she tried to move — but she couldn't, she simply couldn't!

"Having problems?" Justin asked her amiably, not breaking stride as he walked by on his way to fetch new equipment from the car.

"I am *so* stiff!" Roberta wailed. "I can't even move. Oh, the pain!" She tried to take another step, then burst out with an explosive sound, half laugh, half cry. She lifted one leg and tried to bend it, then the other, half laughing, half moaning as she did so.

"Naturally you're stiff," Justin commented casually as he walked on by. "All that crouching and digging you did yesterday, using muscles you probably haven't used for years, if ever. But don't worry about it, it'll soon wear off. At least you're not sunburned on top of it, as poor Coffer is."

Staring after Justin as he walked on by, Roberta felt a hot wave of irritation at his cheerful indifference, but this soon melted away as she remembered what Bill had said yesterday. If only she could be more like Justin, strong, imperturbable, invulnerable! Oh, well, he'd said the stiffness wouldn't last long. Hopefully he would be right. Gritting her teeth against the pain, Roberta struggled to bend down again to grab hold of her sleeping bag and roll it up.

To Roberta's great surprise, the stiffness didn't last too long, or at least stopped being painful enough to bother her. By the time she'd gone to the riverbank to complete her morning's ablutions — wading out to wash herself where the river current ran freely — and had carried a load of material down to the raft at Justin's request, she found to her amazement that she could move quite freely, not hurting too much. Of course, bending was a problem, crouching down next to impossible, but Justin was right again; the stiffness was nothing in particular to worry about and would in time go away. Meanwhile she could cope well enough.

From that morning on, the days tended to melt into each other with little change; measuring, digging, collecting, labeling, she and Bill working on the ground while Justin worked over their heads in the trees, gathering tree scrapings for laboratory analysis. Approximately every three to four days, usually in the early morning, Justin would dictate memos to her for a couple of hours, which she'd type up on the portable typewriter he'd brought along, then one of them, usually Bill, would be designated to drive down to Port Antonio to post their mail and ship their trays to the laboratory in Miami.

They woke with the sun and started each day with a huge breakfast, most often composed of native Jamaican food brought to them, by arrangement, by the black men who had rented them the raft. They ate fruits of every kind: mangoes, bananas, pineapples, guavas, papayas, avocados (called *pears* by the Jamaicans), and of course coconut, with bread, coffee, and tea — an herbal tea brewed from wild herbs growing underfoot. Some days they broke for lunch and sat around companionably at noon having a bite; other days they worked right through. Each workday invariably ended with another large, very satisfactory meal, often eaten on the porch of the house in which the wives of the Jamaican men prepared it for them: sweet potatoes, breadfruit, cabbage, carrots, onions, green beans, tomatoes — these vegetables most often made into soup; hot or cold curries; on occasion, curried goat with rice; sometimes rice with chicken, beef, or pork; almost all the dishes highly spiced and, Roberta thought, mouth-wateringly delicious. She had never had such a huge appetite or eaten so ravenously.

With the day's work done and dinner eaten, for recreation she and Bill would listen to a battery-operated tape player he had brought with him, leaning comfortably against coconut palms as they enjoyed the music on the tapes, or they would play an occasional game of cards, or often they would just sit happily relaxed and talk together. Justin, of course, spent his evenings, as long as there was a glimmer of daylight left, reading endless reports and pamphlets, sometimes continuing even after dark: he'd bend over his books, glasses perched securely on his nose, using a flashlight to read by.

Talk about a one-track mind! Roberta often thought, irritably glancing Justin's way. But then her heartbeat would quicken suddenly with the thought that apparently, at times, Justin did have other thoughts; after all, he was scheduled to get married the moment this assignment ended, and Mrs. Andrews, back in Los Angeles, had commented that he seemed devoted to his fiancée and had refused to sign a contract for longer than three months as that would have interfered with his wedding plans. Just because work was all he thought of when out in the wilds like this accompanied only by his '*fellow employees*' didn't mean there wasn't another side to Justin Martin.

Sighing, Roberta did her best to drop this line of thought and turn her attention back to Bill.

In their long, relaxed evenings together, as she and Bill became more and more companionably at ease with each other, Bill began entertaining her with a repertoire of truly funny stories, or at least they seemed funny the way Bill told them, with his long, freckled face and mournful air. On more than one occasion, laughing until her sides hurt and tears came into her eyes, Roberta commented, "Oh, Bill, you've missed your calling, you really have; you should have become a stand-up comic!" On occasion even Justin would smile or burst out laughing, in spite of sitting yards away reading his endless books. Whenever this happened, whenever Justin, grinning or laughing, would glance over to show them he had heard and thought Bill's story a funny one, Roberta would feel instant pleasure flow through her at the thought that Justin wasn't as far away from them in thought as he often seemed. At the same time, though, he wasn't exactly with them either.

As each day drew to an end, Roberta faced the fact that she had never been so thoroughly deep-down relaxed and happy in her life. Not only did she enjoy the work and the company she was keeping, but for another thing she was becoming acquainted with her own body and using it in a way she never had before, in a way it had never occurred to her to become acquainted with it or use it before. As a girl in school, she had never been in the least athletic; as she'd entered junior high, she had also entered into a period of very fast growth and hadn't seemed able to achieve sufficient coordination to become skilled at any athletic endeavor. Chalking herself off as hopelessly inept, she had never again put any effort into physical activities; she had never, once she left school, taken up any kind of sporting activity, not even tennis, bowling, or swimming. Back home in Los Angeles she had used her body solely as a vehicle to move her from place to place, to walk here, sit there, get her job done, go to the movies, walk around the kitchen fixing dinner, go to bed, not even realizing that a body can be more than a utilitarian runabout. Properly utilized, it can be a continuing source of pleasure and pride.

For the first time in her life Roberta became aware of this, working with Justin and Bill on the riverbank. It became a marvelous pleasure to plunge into the river, an entirely different experience depending on the time of day. The quick wake-me-up splash in the morning was nothing like the midday cool-me-off dive, and neither was the same as the cleansing, relaxing, exhilarating swim of the early evening after the workday was over, when she could slip into the warm currents of the river and give herself up to the sensuous joy of the fading light and the warm embrace of the softly flowing water, a type of pleasure she had never conceived of before.

The first time Roberta swam across the river to the sandbar to wash her clothes, which were tied around her middle as she dog-paddled holding aloft in one arm a box of soap, she felt full-to-bursting with a sense of closeness to the Jamaican women she had by now seen several times on the same sandbar washing their clothes. As she reached the bar and glanced down to find Jamaican women there again, doing the same thing she planned to do, she thought about walking down to ask for instructions, but then with a sigh she thought better of it. They might feel she was intruding; she might disturb the lovely balance of their working or upset their black-skinned children romping on the stones around them, dressed either in colorful shorts or wearing no clothes at all. No, she shouldn't bother them; besides, what was there to know? From time immemorial women had washed clothes this way, using rocks on a riverbank; she knew how to do it instinctively. So untying her dirty clothes, she settled down into a crouch alongside the river to get to work.

As she worked, Roberta smiled to herself, feeling so in love with the world, especially with the lovely spot where she found herself, she could hardly contain herself. Glancing up, she let her eyes feast on the bright green tropical growth on the bank of the river across from her. The air was so clear and clean, the sky such an unclouded blue, the river water was splashing across her hands so refreshing and cool.

Earlier, when she'd gathered her clothes and was making preparations to cross to the bar, Bill approached her, his dirty clothes tied into a tight little bundle. "Roberta, I don't suppose you'd be willing — I mean, I really don't have much of a knack for that kind of thing — " he said, hesitantly extending his bundle toward her. Even here in the wilderness, where she was doing as much work as Bill was, and exactly the same work, still it was women's work to wash clothes, wasn't it?

Although she'd half reached out to take the bundle, something in Roberta didn't like it. She wanted to rebel and tell Bill, tell him sharply, to get busy and wash his own clothes, that it wasn't her responsibility to take care of his personal needs. But before she said anything, before she'd quite decided what she would do, Justin, to her surprise, hurried over.

"What's that you're saying?" Justin snapped, walking over to them. Justin said quickly, with an angry flatness to his voice, "Around here, everyone pulls his own weight. No one sloughs off his personal responsibilities onto someone else, is that understood? Are you reading me, Coffer?"

His freckled cheeks staining a bright red, Bill muttered, hastily trying to hide the bundle of clothes behind his back, "Righto, chief," and he quickly turned then and walked away, taking his dirty clothes with him.

A few minutes after she'd settled down on the sandbar to begin washing, Roberta saw Justin swim across, followed not long after by Bill. She handed Justin the box of soap as he reached her, which he accepted with a grin, and walking down the sandbar some fifteen feet, he settled down to do his own dirty wash.

Shortly after, Bill climbed onto the sandbar, helped himself to some soap from the box Justin had, and settled down to do his own washing while Roberta smiled to herself.

Before their three-week stay on the riverbank ended, it came out that Justin wasn't completely invulnerable after all. On their very first day there — the day they'd hired the raft and started down the river, accidentally spilling over — the force of the spill had thrown Justin down onto rocks barely under the surface of the water and he had suffered a severe gash on the right shin, which bled quite profusely. After bandaging the leg, Justin had seemed to give it no further thought, so Roberta and Bill had dismissed thought of it too. Each morning Justin would rebandage his lower leg with the same businesslike efficiency with which he did everything else, and for the first week the cut seemed to be healing nicely, giving no problem. But on their eighth day on the river, one late afternoon when Justin was shinnying up a palm, Roberta and Bill suddenly heard him cry out an angry expletive. When they called up in alarm to ask what had happened, Justin called back that it was nothing, to please excuse his language, everything was fine. After exchanging a worried frown, Roberta and Bill could do little but shrug it off and return to work.

When Justin reached the ground sometime later they learned that in climbing the palm he had caught his bandage on a rough spot, the bandage had been ripped off, and he had reopened his cut; once again it was bleeding profusely. "No matter," Justin declared in his usual, no-nonsense voice. "I'll just bind it up again and it will be fine."

In the days that followed, however, it turned out not to be fine. The wound, reopened, began to fester; the gash seemed to deepen and become infected. For several days Justin continued to maintain that the leg was no problem;

he applied salves, disinfectants, bandaged the leg, and went about business as usual, shinnying up one tree after another just as he had done from the start. But by their sixteenth day on the river he could keep it up no longer. He was limping noticeably as he walked and was in obvious pain. The cut simply wasn't healing properly and, Justin finally admitted, probably wouldn't heal as long as he continued to subject it to the continual abuse of being rubbed against the bark of the palms as he climbed.

"I'm sorry to have to do this to you, Coffer," Justin said at noon that day, scowling, "but I'm afraid you'll have to take over for me for a day or two. It's quite simple, really, and I'm sure that in no time at all you'll get the hang of it."

Roberta, who'd been standing watching Justin's face, one hand lifted to shield her eyes, glanced quickly around at Bill. Though it seemed to her that his freckled face paled slightly, he made no objection; in fact, he even managed to force out a nervous grin.

"Whatever you say," Bill said agreeably, though his voice sounded a slight bit shaky under the forced hardiness. "Just give me a few hints on how to do it and I'm sure I'll do fine."

"I'm sure you will too," Justin said. As Roberta half turned away to return to her own task, Justin said quickly, "Roberta, you might as well listen, too, just in case," so she turned back to listen as instructed.

Just in case what? Roberta wondered. As Justin gave Bill instructions about climbing the palms, she glanced up at the one they stood near, towering overhead one hundred feet in the air, and felt herself shiver with gratitude that it was Bill and not she who had to climb it. Heights, even moderate heights, had always given her the willies; she had never cared for 'thrill' rides such as roller coasters or Ferris wheels. In fact, no one had ever been able to lure her onto either one. She preferred to keep both feet firmly planted on the solid ground at all times, in all places. But Bill, though he looked a bit pale and nervous perhaps, didn't seem really to mind having to climb.

Justin removed the spurs from his own boots, knelt down and fastened them onto Bill's. Standing again, smiling, he undid the body belt he wore and slipped that around Bill, fastening it. He showed Bill how to knot the rope he'd be using, explained to him how to draw it taut, how loose to keep it as he climbed. "Just go up like a telephone linesman would; it's much the same climb," Justin said cheerfully. Giving Bill a hearty clap on the shoulder, saying, "That's the way," he walked with him to the foot of the palm, threw the rope around the trunk, fastened the free end onto the body belt Bill now wore, and said, "There you go." After a long lingering glance up the tree, Bill began climbing.

Tensing, Roberta swung away to

return to her dig, but realized that Justin wasn't turning to join her. Instead he stood a few feet from the base of the palm watching Bill climb, his handsome face caught in a worried scowl. "That's the way, that's the way," she heard him murmur repeatedly to himself, as though the force of his will was needed to keep Bill going. Roberta stopped walking and turned to watch Bill herself, a deepening frown darkening her face.

Bill, about eighteen feet up by then, seemed to be slowing in this upward progress. He'd ease the rope up, pause, run his arm across his forehead; finally, slowly, move one foot up, then the other; then again he'd pause, running his arm over his forehead, do nothing, fool with the rope, run his arm across his forehead, stop moving entirely, test the rope, run his other arm across his forehead — then suddenly Roberta was aware that when Bill next worked with the rope, it was not to move it up on the palm. Rather, he was sliding it down, easing it down; he was climbing down.

"Damn!" Justin exploded under his breath, stepping over toward the base of the tree. He stood staring up his dark eyes blazing, as Bill slowly and awkwardly descended the last few feet. Reaching the ground Bill unfastened the body belt and stepped away from it, putting a couple of feet between himself and Justin before facing him.

"Sorry, Mr. Martin, truly I am," the freckled redhead muttered, his splotchy sunburned face running sweat. He ran an arm across his forehead again, nervously trying to stop the rivers of sweat running down his cheeks. "but — well, I just couldn't make it, that's all. Dizziness, nausea — I just couldn't do it. I wanted to, I tried, you saw me try, but I just couldn't. Sorry again."

Looking suddenly green, Bill swung around, staggered about ten feet away, then leaning over began to vomit, his thin frame shaking. Poor guy, Roberta thought, hating to see him in such obvious misery.

"No matter," Justin said crisply. He stood a moment holding the body belt as though half of a mind to slap it on himself again, never mind that the slash on his shin was festering so badly he couldn't even walk without limping anymore. But after swinging it half into place, he suddenly looked around at Roberta instead and said, in his cheerful, clipped voice, "How about you, Roberta, want to give it a try? Somebody's got to go up there to get those scrapings."

With an immediate nervous smile Roberta opened her mouth to say she was sorry, heights bothered her; there was no way she could climb. After all, Justin wasn't ordering her to do it as he'd earlier ordered Bill; he was merely asking her, with a half-teasing little smile at that, as though he fully expected her to shake her head in answer and murmur no, laughing — a private little joke between them.

Either Justin could revise his plans and they simply wouldn't get scrapings from any more palms, or Justin himself could continue climbing — subjecting his infected cut to even more trauma, possibly risking serious consequences. Suddenly shaking, Roberta stepped foward, still smiling.

"Well, I — I'm willing to give it a try, I guess," she stammered, unable to believe she was actually saying any such thing. Was she out of her mind?

"Good girl!" Justin exclaimd, his dark eyes flashing with pleasure, and as he laughed Roberta laughed too. This was all just a big joke, right? Any minute now Justin would realize she was only kidding and she'd be safely out of it again!

As she stepped up to him, Justin took hold of her by the shoulders — how firm yet gentle his touch was! — and maneuvered her around a bit to get the body belt on her. Excusing himself, he limped hurriedly over to where Bill now lay sprawled on the ground, face down, and said, "Excuse me, old man, but I need the spurs; Roberta's going to give it a try," and within a minute he was back, kneeling down before Roberta, fastening the climbing spurs onto her boots. Straightening up again, he grinned at her and she smiled back, telling herself she didn't really feel scared, didn't really feel so sick to her stomach already that if she didn't watch out she'd start to retch. Which was utterly absurd — at this point she still had both feet firmly in contact with the ground!

"Did you follow the instructions I was earlier giving Bill?" Justin asked, in his usual clipped voice; yet somehow it seemed edged now both with warmth and solicitude.

Nodding nervously in answer, afraid to trust her voice, which would surely quiver and break if she tried to speak, Roberta allowed herself to be gently turned to face the palm. Justin slung the rope around it, fastened it to her belt, gave her a few parting words of instruction, a friendly smile, a pat on the shoulder — and away she was supposed to go, one hundred feet straight up!

Swallowing painfully, Roberta lifted one foot and took her first step up; she lifted the other foot and she was on her way. Just don't look down! she kept telling herself; you'll do just fine as long as you don't look down! Wiggling the rope up, keeping it just taut enough, lifting one foot, digging the spurs in, lifting the other foot, digging the spurs in, higher and higher . . .

Oh, she was surely going to faint! If she stopped to think where she was, what she was doing . . . But that was something else she mustn't do, mustn't think, mustn't look down, mustn't notice how panicked she felt, sweat popping out on her brow; mustn't pay any attention to how terribly nauseated she was, to how she had to swallow hard every other minute to keep it down — had she gone up as far as Bill had before giving up? If she got up as far as he did, then she wouldn't be any more disgraced than he'd been if she had to give up and climb back down. How high up was she? But if she looked down to find out — or looked up . . . Oh, she couldn't bear to look either way! What in the world was she doing up here anyway?

And then she heard Justin's voice calling up to her, not to tell her to forget the whole thing and come back down, not to tell her to be careful so as not to get hurt, not to tell her he cared too much for her to subject her to this much stress. Instead he called out, his voice crisp yet joyful, "That's the way, Roberta, you're doing just great!" which made her feel instantly furious at him.

Little he knew how she was doing, whether she was doing well or poorly, and the fact of the matter was he cared even less! As long as she kept going, moving the rope, lifting one foot, then the other, moving the rope, on and on, up and up, higher and higher — little he cared how she felt about it as long as she kept going, kept climbing, didn't give up! So don't look, don't think, just keep moving! Roberta kept ordering herself, half relieved, half even more furious that Justin didn't call up to her a second time. By now he probably wasn't even watching her, by now he had probably dismissed all thought of her! Did he care why she had agreed to do this, that she was doing it out of consideration for him, to keep him from climbing any more with that badly infected cut? All he cared about was their work, getting scrapings from these palms, tracking down the cause of the blight. That was all that cold, thoughtless, arrogant man cared about, forcing her to climb like this!

And then suddenly, miraculously, she was there, reaching the leaves at the top of the tree, close to a hundred feet off the ground! She had done it!

For the first time, after taking a deep, deep breath, Roberta dared to look down. And there was Justin a tiny little figure down there at the base of the palm, staring up at her, waving. Abruptly grinning, Roberta lifted her eyes and looked around, suddenly no longer frightened. Why, this was no worse than being up in the sky in a plane, and flying had never bothered her. The fact was it was lovely, with the clear blue sky overhead, a light, cool breeze stirring through the leaves of the palm, herself securely fastened in by her body belt and rope so that she couldn't possibly fall. With a little laugh she drew out the knife from her belt and began making the scrapings that Justin had sent her up here to get, carefully depositing each scraping in the narrow tray suspended from her neck which had been put there for that purpose. As she worked she began singing softly to herself, forgetting completely about where she was.

Climbing back down some time later, she knew she had made the climb not only for Justin but for herself, for herself even more than for him. She had proven to herself that she could do something that took courage and skill, and she was ecstatic.

As she reached the ground at last, Justin, who'd been standing watching her descend from a few feet back, took quick strides over to reach her, grinning, throwing one arm around her shoulders.

"Good sport!" he said, momentarily squeezing her to him, and for that moment at least, while maybe still not aware of her as a woman, he was at least aware of her as a person, as someone he liked and respected, which at least was a start, wasn't it?

But . . . a start on what?

4

ON the morning of their twenty-first day on the river, Justin announced that they had completed their work in the area and therefore would pack up the car and drive back to Kingston to enjoy a few days off.

"It may not seem like it," Justin said, "but we've really accomplished a great deal and deserve some rest. I'm really proud of the way you two have pitched in and worked."

"Like slaves," Bill Coffer muttered under his breath to Roberta, which brought forth an immediate answering grin from her. They *had* worked hard, yes, but at the same time she had never enjoyed herself so much in her life.

After they'd packed the car, Justin drove them down the narrow mountain road with the same daredevil skill he'd shown before, but this time Roberta scarcely batted an eye; somehow it seemed only right to travel that way, speeding, swerving, darting, never braking unless absolutely forced to. She sat gazing out the window, completely relaxed. In just three weeks her companions had become an integral part of her life — and so many happy, busy weeks still stretched out before them. That the three months would ever draw to an end, that she would ever have to leave here and return to her former life, no longer seemed a possibility. Now, *this* now, would simply go on forever. So she could sit in the car utterly relaxed and gaze idly out the window at the fiercely bright tropical landscape as Justin wildly drove them home.

Arriving at the Sheraton-Kingston, each took his own belongings and retired to his own room, Justin suggesting that they enjoy time off from each other at least until dinner. Walking into her room, Roberta grinned in relief.

How glad she was to see it again, the bed, fresh clothing, and especially the bathroom! Within minutes she had shed her sticky, sweaty clothes and was luxuriating in a tubful of cool water, telling herself that she could happily lie right there for the rest of the afternoon.

But she hadn't been in the tub five minutes when she heard a loud pounding on her bedroom door. She sat upright, thinking to herself that of course she would have to climb out of the tub, wrap up in a towel, and go find out who was there; but then she thought to herself that it couldn't possibly be anyone important, and whoever it was could just pound away until he got tired and left. Justin had said specifically that he wouldn't see her again until evening and so had Bill, so why should she answer the door?

Sinking back down in the cool water, Roberta tried to shut the sound of the pounding out.

Two more hard raps, then silence. Two minutes later the pounding started again, even louder than before, then again it stopped. But the next thing Roberta knew she was sure she heard steps across her bedroom floor, then a tap on the bathroom door, which stood partly open.

"Who's there?" Who would dare enter her room uninvited like that?

"Roberta, it's me," Justin's voice said. "Something's come up, something terribly exciting, I think. Grab a robe and come out so I can tell you about it, all right?"

"All right." Her heart pounding in spite of herself, Roberta pushed the door shut and quickly climbed out of the tub. Hastily drying herself, she grabbed her robe, drew it on, and hurried out the door.

Justin stood in the middle of her room, his back to her. He swung around immediately, flashing her the most delightfully boyish grin she had ever seen.

"Guess what, Roberta? When I went to the desk just now to check us back in, I was given a message that came in a couple of days ago. A very dear friend of mine, my fiancée in fact, arrived in Ocho Rios, Jamaica, a couple of days ago. I've already called the airport and made arrangements to fly over in thirty minutes. Want to go along?"

As her eyes met his, Roberta felt her heart sink. Somehow over the past three weeks she had managed to forget what she knew perfectly well to be true: that Justin belonged to someone else. She had never managed to actually persuade herself, even in her most self-deluded moments, that he had secretly fallen in love with her, but still he *had* almost seemed to be hers, at least for the duration of their assignment. To be slapped in the face with harsh reality so quickly, when she'd been feeling so happy . . . How cold and tired and dispirited she suddenly felt!

"Well, I don't know, Justin. I mean — what would be the point of my going along? If you're flying over to see your fiancée — "

"But Ocho Rios is a truly lovely port, far nicer than anything here in Kingston. Besides, it will be Christmas in another few days, I think we all deserve a little time off. I've already asked Bill and he says he'd like to go if you want to."

"Well, I — I really don't know."

Justin's boyish grin faded away and he turned to leave. "Suit yourself, of course," he said, in his crisp clipped voice. "But I really think you'd be making a mistake to turn this down. The four of us could see the sights together, with plenty of time in between to rest and sleep. Just say the word and I'll phone over for reservations."

To spend her time off not just with Justin, but with Justin accompanied by his fiancée . . . Oh, didn't he realize that was simply asking too much of her? That moment she felt overwhelmed with fatigue; for three weeks they had put in ten- to twelve-hour days with scarcely an hour off in between, much less a full day — and now to be faced with this . . . How had she let herself fall into such a terrible trap?

She had allowed herself to believe, to hope, to fantasize, deliberately ignoring the facts. In spite of the three weeks they had just spent working together, Justin was the same man she had first met in Los Angeles, a man in love, looking forward to his forthcoming marriage. And as much as she felt inside that she'd changed, she was in fact still the same woman: Roberta Somers, thin, bony, unattractive. Roberta shivered, cold tears coming into her eyes. To Justin she was still just a fellow employee; she would never be anything else. If she couldn't learn to adjust to that . . .

"Well, what do you say?" Justin asked, his eyes circling around to face her again. "Will you come or won't you? To make arrangements I need to know."

As Roberta's eyes met his, her heart

abruptly gave a wild little flip, for deep in Justin's eyes it seemed to her . . . No, no, he couldn't possibly really care; he was just being polite, courteous, trying to be fair to a fellow employee who had worked very hard! He couldn't possibly really care whether or not she went along; yet there in his eyes, deep down inside his dark, dark eyes there was something . . .

"Well, all right," Roberta said. "Tell Bill if he wants to go, I'll go too."

"Good enough!" Justin exclaimed with a smile. "That's great. I'll go phone for rooms and meet you downstairs in twenty minutes." He stepped across the threshold, began to pull the door closed, but then hesitated and looked back. His eyes meeting Roberta's, he said in a warm, soft voice, "Roberta, I'm truly glad," before he closed the door and disappeared. What a darling he was!

Just a few minutes before, upon entering this room, she had vowed she wouldn't leave it again for hours, that she would soak in the tub for hours, and then stretch out on top of her lovely, smooth bed. But here she was, just minutes later, hurrying to dress, to pack a case and rush out to the airport.

Roberta grinned to herself, then burst out with a soft, happy laugh. Justin was glad she was going; he had actually said so in so many words. And she was glad too.

In twenty minutes she was ready, down in the main lobby waiting for Justin and Bill, neither of whom did she see anywhere. But she'd been there less than a minute when the two men came striding up, Justin with an excited smile playing around his mouth, Bill's brightly freckled, sunburned face caught in its usual mournful expression.

All too soon, having taken a taxi to the airport, they were climbing into a small, four-passenger plane that would have terrified Roberta to fly in a mere month before; to her eyes it looked as old, rickety, and insubstantial as the plane the Wright brothers flew in, long before she was born.

"Hey, you're sure this thing's safe?" Bill asked nervously as Justin settled down behind the controls, signaling for Bill and Roberta to make themselves comfortable in the passenger seats behind him.

"Of course it's safe," Justin replied good-naturedly, "as safe as anything ever is. Nothing in life's ever guaranteed, so why worry about it, right?" With these reassuring words, he yanked out the throttle, worked with various controls, and the engine started up, noisily prohibiting further conversation.

"This is the only neck I've got; that's why I worry," Bill muttered morosely to Roberta, leaning over close to drop the words directly into her ear, causing Roberta to laugh softly to herself. What a worrywart Bill Coffer was!

The flight was such a short one it seemed as though they were barely in the air before Justin was descending again to land them rather bouncily at an airstrip in Ocho Rios. As he shut off the engine he swung around, grinning, dark eyes flashing. "There. I told you it was perfectly safe. In no time we'll be settling into our rooms at the Hilton and Roberta can climb back into the tub and finish off the bath I interrupted in Kingston." As Justin laughed, Roberta laughed too, irresistibly carried along by Justin's overflowing good humor. How glad she was she'd decided to come!

Once shown to her lovely private room at the Hilton, Roberta stood for a moment glancing around, then decided that what she would most enjoy at this point was a nap. It was a little after three and in all probability she wouldn't see either Justin or Bill again until evening, for dinner. She began to undress and, after pulling on a light robe, she turned down her bed and climbed into it. After three weeks of back-breaking work, it was heavenly to have these few days off.

At six-thirty her phone rang, and

Justin informed her that he'd meet her and Bill in the lobby at seven. "I hope it's all right," Justin said, "but I've already mapped out an evening for us, one that I feel we'll all enjoy. I figured that since both you and Bill are new in the country while I've been here before — "

"Of course, that's fine," Roberta said. "See you then." She hung up happily, growing more excited by the moment at the thought of the evening ahead.

Before dressing, she ruefully looked over her meager wardrobe, but she really had next-to-no choice as to what she would wear. She had brought only one dress from home and, while hurriedly packing that afternoon, had decided against bringing it along on this trip; to her critical eye it had suddenly looked too shapeless and drab ever to wear again. The fact was that, even though at home she'd considered it her very best dress — the most expensive one she'd ever owned — it was a dull dark brown, had never fit too well, and in her heart she guessed she had always loathed it. It really was fit for little else then to wear to funerals, which is what she had bought it for in the first place, to wear to her mother's funeral two years before. A modest, well-made, practical dress — but she was through dressing that way, Roberta had decided, and in a fit of scorn had left her one dress behind, hanging in the closet of her room in Kingston.

Instead she had brought both of her pants suits. Now she set each suit out on the bed and looked each one over, the dark blue one she'd worn the morning she'd first met Justin back in the home office, and the dark green one she'd worn on the plane. Some choice! Neither had ever rated a second glance from any man, and Justin had already seen them both. Oh, well, what possible difference did it make?

Sighing, Roberta decided on the blue, which possibly fit a bit better. Pulling on the slacks, then glancing at herself critically in a full-length door mirror, she was surprised and pleased to see that they seemed to fit better than ever. Over these past three weeks, eating as ravenously as she had, she had apparently put on some weight! Heart instantly lifting, she pulled out a blouse from her bag — a wildly patterned cotton one she had bought in Port Antonio one day — and after giving it a couple of shakes she pulled it on. Turning this way and that in front of the mirror, Roberta suddenly smiled at her reflection. How tanned and glowing her face looked! And she loved the bright colors of the native shirt! After a moment she grabbed up the suit jacket and pulled that on, again looking critically at herself. Well, so she wasn't the most gorgeous fashion model in the world, but, in her own eyes at least, she looked pretty good.

A few minutes later Roberta stepped through her door, out into the corridor. Bill, who was on a different floor, had phoned her to say that he was going down to the lounge for a while and would meet her and Justin in the lobby at seven. Bill, herself, Justin — and Justin's fiancée. Oh, well, few things in life are ever perfect.

Straightening her shoulders, feeling a wonderful deep sense of well-being, Roberta started off down the hall. A moment later she was startled to hear her name, and glancing quickly around, she saw it was Justin, who was striding rapidly up to her with a broad grin on his face. Dressed in a black turtleneck sweater and black corduroy slacks — the clothes he had worn on their flight from home — he looked so attractive she felt her pulse give a frightened leap.

"Hey, you look great!" Justin said, reaching her. His fingers touched her elbow, then took hold and held her arm as they walked forward. "In fact, you look better than great, you look fantastic. If ever I saw a living, breathing advertisement for the value of hard work and healthy outdoor living, you're it. You've put on a little weight, haven't you?"

Her cheeks blushing warmly, Roberta murmured, "Yes, I think so," though it was quite beyond her to face Justin directly as his eyes swept appreciatively over her. His fingers on her forearm seemed to exert a slight loving pressure. How frighteningly close he was. If only things were different.

They reached the elevator. Justin's hand dropped away and he backed off a step, his eyes seeking hers. Glancing around at him, Roberta felt her heart drop dismally at his suddenly grim expression.

"Roberta, I sincerely apologize." Justin's voice was thin and stiff; his eyes moved off. "Back at the start of this assignment I gave you my word I'd never think of you other than as a fellow employee, and I had no business saying what I just did or even noticing how you look." Justin paused, then added, his eyes circling back, "So I do hope you'll forget I ever said it and will continue to trust me, a trust I'll prove worthy of, believe me."

Face burning, heart pounding wildly, Roberta murmured, "Of course, Justin, if you like," though her heart pinched in pain over his words. The elevator arrived and they both stepped in.

Two floors below, Justin left the elevator again, saying he was going for Alicia and would see her and Bill down in the lobby. "You'll both like Alicia, I'm sure," he said, stepping out and striding quickly away.

Bill, dressed in dark green slacks and an open-necked light green shirt, looked very nice, Roberta thought. His face lit with pleasure as she approached, and he hurried to meet her, his hand reaching out to take her arm.

"Wish it were just the two of us going out," he muttered anxiously, big orange freckles bouncing across his face. "It's bad enough having to be with Justin; I'll be a nervous wreck having his fiancée with us too. She's some big-shot heiress or something. At

143

least," Bill ended morosely, drawing out a handkerchief to wipe his damp brow, "she's one of the jet-setters, maybe an actress or model, I don't know. But who needs someone like that around?"

Smiling, Roberta said firmly, "You won't be a nervous wreck, Bill, you'll be fine. And obviously, from what you've just said, you don't really know a thing about Alicia, so let's not jump to a lot of wild conclusions, all right? All either of us knows is that she's the woman Justin's going to marry and she's come here to pay him a visit. And I'm sure," Roberta ended in a firm, confident voice, while feeling anything but sure of what she was saying, "that we'll both like her very much and thoroughly enjoy our evening with them. So what do you say you wipe off that scowl and act happy for a change?"

Bill's light eyes met hers; he stared mournfully at her a moment, then a nervous grin broke across his face and his hand squeezed her arm. "You're right, of course, Roberta, as you always are. You're one great woman, do you know that?"

"Why, thank you, kind sir," Roberta answered.

"I mean that," Bill said earnestly. "I feel that by now I know you quite well and in my opinion you're the greatest. But I know I'm not going to like Alicia whatever-her-name-is no matter what you say."

Grinning companionably, Roberta said, "All right, don't like her, but for Pete's sake relax and enjoy yourself anyway. We're out to have a good time!"

Though they'd never known Justin, a demon for punctuality, to be late before, he didn't arrive in the lobby until close to seven-thirty. But Roberta, her heart pounding wildly as she saw him at last, knew perfectly well that it wasn't Justin's fault. Alicia had unquestionably kept him waiting. The two of them, Justin and his fiancée, stepped off the elevator and began walking across the lobby, eyes fastened on each other as they talked and laughed. Roberta had heard from the start that Alicia Markham was a beautiful woman, but still she wasn't prepared for what she saw: a young blond woman so extraordinarily lovely that every pair of eyes swung to stare at her, to feast on the sight of her, as Justin was feasting his eyes hungrily on her. No wonder he'd been so excited about coming here to see her!

"Alicia, darling, my co-workers, Roberta Somers and Bill Coffer," Justin said, coming to a stop before them. "Roberta, Bill, my fiancée Alicia Markham." Justin's voice, saying his fiancée's name, seemed to take on a different note, a note of bursting pride and delight. *This is the woman I love, the woman I adore!* his voice and expression said, glowing with it. Roberta's heart instantly ached so painfully that she could feel tears of frustration and longing edge into her eyes.

"How do you do, Miss Markham?" she said, trying to sound as warm and friendly as she could. That she had dared even to secretly yearn for a man engaged to a woman who looked like this seemed ridiculous.

"How do *you* do, Roberta?" Alicia Markham said, smiling, reaching for Roberta's right hand with both of hers, holding and squeezing it. "Justin's told me about you, in both letters and over the phone, and it's so nice to meet you at last. And you too, Bill."

Turning her attention to Bill, Alicia reached for his hand next, smiling up at him. A woman of medium height, she had soft blond hair, wide-set, large blue eyes, glowing skin, and a figure that was truly sensational.

Remembering the pleasure she'd earlier felt in her own somewhat improved appearance, Roberta wanted to run and hide, to find herself a corner somewhere to cry in. So she'd put on a becoming pound or two — she still looked like a dried-out prune compared to the lovely, curvacious Alicia, who, in the low-cut pale yellow dress she wore, looked like a fully ripe peach all but bursting its skin. No wonder every man in the room kept turning to stare at her!

As they walked outside to get a taxi, Bill, walking alongside Roberta, whispered gleefully, "Hey, Roberta, once again you were right. Alicia's okay. Already I can tell she's the kind of person I'm going to enjoy being with. If only I could learn not to worry so much ahead of time!"

If only I could learn not to be so happy ahead of time! Roberta thought in echo, remembering how pleased she had been that Justin had seemed really to want her to come along, remembering even more clearly the way his eyes had lit up at sight of her in the corridor outside her room, his voice telling her how nice she looked. When would she finally get over the impossible hope that one day Justin would look at her as a woman and find her worth loving? He already had a woman to love. It was time that once and for all she came to her senses and grew up!

Justin had made dinner reservations for them at the Tower Isle Hotel.

"From what I hear, we'll be able to get a civilized meal there," Alicia remarked sweetly in the cab going over. She sat beside Justin in the back seat, close to him, her arm possessively wound through his, but glanced around at Roberta, sitting on her other side, as she spoke. "French cooking is really the only food worth eating, don't you agree?" she said with a soft sweet smile.

Feeling exceedingly uncomfortable, Roberta murmured, "Well, quite possibly you're right, I really don't know," and a moment later turned her eyes away to sit gazing out the car window. Bill sat beside the driver in front, sitting stiffly upright, looking about as relaxed and comfortable as she felt. Bill had been right — what a horror of an evening lay ahead!

At the restaurant, Roberta saw a new side to Justin, one she had supposed was there but hadn't been exposed to before: the suave sophisticate completely at home with an international menu which was totally foreign to Roberta. She couldn't make any sense of it, and as she sat looking it over she began to feel so uncomfortable that she felt sick, and so angry at herself for feeling this way that she wanted to scream. Not even Bill's presence at her side was any help; rather, he only made things worse, continually fidgeting, and the one time she glanced around at him his face looked so green-tinged under his freckles she'd immediately been struck by the horrified fear that he might lose control and do something awful, like having to bolt from the table to vomit, or even worse, not bolt from the table when nausea overwhelmed him and he had to vomit! Then suddenly Roberta felt saved.

Justin leaned over toward her, so incredibly handsome in his dark turtle-neck sweater, his dark eyes flashing merrily in his deeply suntanned face. "Roberta, if I may — may I order for you? That's something I always greatly enjoy doing, introducing my friends to gastronomic delights that possibly will be new to them. If you'd trust me in this, as you've already trusted me in other ways — what do you say?"

As his boyish grin broke across his painfully handsome face, Roberta felt suddenly faint, but safely rescued too.

"That would be fine, thank you." She reclosed the menu as her cheeks flushed lightly. "Possibly Bill too. Why don't you let Justin do the honors for both of us?" Roberta suggested to the redhead.

"Hey, great," Bill said, and hastily folded his own menu back up.

"In that case," Alicia remarked, glancing around at Justin — with a slightly peevish look? Roberta wondered — "why don't you order for me also?

I'm sure that whatever you chose for our guests will be fine with me." She smiled across the table at Roberta and Bill.

A slight look of surprise lit up Justin's eyes, but with a smile and nod he acknowledged her request, and when the waiter came over he ordered identical dinners for all of them: *Salade de melon et jambon, Soupe à l'oignon, Canard à l'orange* with *Pommes Parisienne* and *Aubergines farcies provençales*, with *Soufflé au citron* for dessert, with red and white wines to be served. After ordering, Justin smiled across at Roberta, who quickly smiled back, beginning to feel somewhat more at ease.

After dinner, which Roberta thoroughly enjoyed, Justin suggested they move on to a nightspot where they could enjoy some authentic Jamaican nightlife. "Of course nothing's really authentic anymore," Justin amended his statement, laughing. "Once the tourists come flooding in, the native culture is

152

never the same again. But even so, we'll get to see some of the native dances — the limbo, the bamboo, the fire dance — and listen to the beat of a reasonably genuine Calypso band. What do you say?"

"Sounds fine," Roberta murmured.

"Okay by me," Bill said, sounding as though he meant it.

"Justin, are you sure you want to?" Alicia objected, with just a slight hint of a childish pout. "Surely you must be tired. From what you've said, it's been a dreadfully long day for you, and for Bill and Roberta too. Shouldn't we just return to the hotel and call it a night?" She turned to smile sweetly at Bill, then at Roberta, as though to make sure neither would take offense.

"Nonsense," Justin said, grinning. "We've got all day tomorrow to catch up on sleep, and the rest of us are raring to go. Just for an hour or so, darling?"

"Well, if you really want to, all right," Alicia graciously gave in, pressing even closer against Justin, smiling up at him. "I was only thinking of how tired you must be, otherwise I'd be happy to go."

"It's all settled then," Justin smiled, and leaning down he pressed a quick friendly kiss on the tip of Alicia's nose, sending a stab of pain through Roberta's heart as she watched. Somehow even a passionate kiss on the mouth wouldn't have hurt quite as much.

They climbed into the cab. Justin gave the driver instructions, and they drove into the dark Jamaican night.

Afterwards Roberta remembered that night largely as a fantastic whirl of splashing color and lights. At the first nightspot they went to, the Club Maracas, Justin persuaded her to sample a native rum drink, which seemed to all but lift the top off her head. Sometime after that they left the club and went to another one, the Brown Jug Club, where Justin, laughing, pushed another rum drink toward her, which she foolishly drank.

Her head was spinning.

The third club they went to was small, crowded, noisy, aflame with brilliant colors and vibrating with the penetrating beat of native music. In the floor show young black men, bare-chested, black skins gleaming, strong young muscles rippling, performed native dances: the bamboo, in which the two dancers facing each other, grace-fully, expertly, rhythmically, skipped over moving bamboo poles, never faltering, never skipping a beat; the limbo, in which they bent their bodies backwards with such incredible control that they could slip under poles held barely inches from the floor; and the fire dance, in which a young Jamaican man whirled lit torches around as he danced, then drew the flame into his mouth, exhaling it out again. Roberta sat entranced, head whirling, never having seen anything like it. And always there was the beat, beat, beat of the music thundering through her.

After the fire dance, the MC of the

floor show tried to lure tourists to come onto the dance floor to join the young natives in the limbo dance. Spotting beautiful blond Alicia sitting alongside Justin at their ringside table, the MC, a slender, wiry, middle-aged Jamaican with a shining gold tooth flashing out when he grinned, came over to her and tried to draw her onto the floor, causing the men in the audience to break into spontaneous cheers and whistles. But Alicia shook her head decisively no. Her set expression showed clearly that she did not feel flattered that the man had noticed her; instead she felt offended.

"How about your gentleman escort then?" the MC suggested, turning quickly to Justin. "You have the look of a sporting man, sir." With that he took hold of Justin's arm, and with a slightly self-conscious grin Justin allowed himself to be led onto the floor.

Three other tourists, a man and two women, joined the two black performers and Justin to try to do the limbo dance.

"Wouldn't you know Superman Martin would give it a try?" Bill leaned close to Roberta to whisper, but in immediate annoyance, Roberta shushed him up. She sat watching with almost pained pleasure as Justin was given instructions by the dancers, as he tried to follow their lead and bend his body over backwards to slide under the pole. How impossibly handsome he looked, with his black hair, deeply tanned face, slender yet powerful body — it was almost more than Roberta could bear to sit there watching him, especially with the lovely Alicia sitting there watching too, her big blue eyes fastened on her fiancée. If *only*, Roberta thought in dismay, but she wouldn't allow herself to finish the thought. It was time she grew up enough to give up impossible dreams!

The other male tourist on the floor wore a wildly colorful native shirt reminiscent of Roberta's, knee-length shorts, and dirty white tennis shoes. He looked about fifty and was quite plump. He knocked the pole down on his first attempt to slide under it, when it was still almost three feet from the floor, which caused the crowd to hoot and roar. The two women, both young and slender, made it under without much strain, then Justin followed, also managing to clear it with relative ease. But as the pole was lowered, each one in turn knocked it down; the MC grinned, the crowd roared. After failing, the two young women tried to leave the floor, as did Justin, but the MC held each one back, insisting that they try again. Both of the young women knocked the pole down a second time, and the MC, with profuse thanks, allowed them to exit from the floor, escaping the spotlight, which left only Justin still to try.

On his second attempt Justin made it under, to the uproarious approval of the crowd.

Grinning, he took a very slight bow, then started off the floor, but once again the MC grabbed his arm and held him back. The two young black performers quickly lowered the pole again, challenging Justin to give it another try. Justin shook his head no, laughing; he could never make it under, he said. The MC put it up to the crowd: shouldn't this supple and powerful young man give it at least one more try?

The crowd roared back a resounding yes.

The MC, holding Justin's arm, pulled him back into position, and Justin gave in. He would try.

He approached the pole, inched forward, lowered himself even more, and at the last minute somehow managed to drop his chest and head even lower, doubling his legs under him. Somehow he made it under the pole with a hairsbreadth to spare.

The patrons in the club, jumping up, shouting, whistling, screaming, roared their approval. The MC rushed around to Justin, grabbing his hand to pump it repeatedly in congratulations. The two young Jamaican dancers, grinning, hurriedly lowerd the pole several inches more, gesturing for Justin to come try again; but, his face now gleaming with perspiration, Justin shook his head decisively no, saying with a grin, "I'll quit now, thank you, while I can still move," and he strode off the floor to another round of whistles and wild applause.

"Hey, that was great!" Bill Coffer exclaimed, standing to shake Justin's hand as he arrived back at the table, his freckled face radiating pleasure.

As Justin sat back down, he leaned over to press a quick kiss on Alicia's cheek, while she quickly drew her chair over closer to put her arm through his.

"I don't know how they dare do that," Alicia murmured, with a slight peevish frown. "Expecting the patrons to get up to entertain like that. We're paying to *be* entertained, not to supply the floor show ourselves. I think you ought to lodge a protest."

Laughing, Justin leaned over to kiss Alicia's cheek a second time, while Roberta lowered her eyes, unable to watch anymore. Justin was fantastic — he was also Alicia's fiancé. It was time she adjusted to that.

The MC announced that the floor show was over, and the floor was cleared for dancing. Justin and Alicia left the table to dance. Roberta did her best not to watch them, but having once seen them together, Roberta knew she would never be able to drive out of her mind, nor out of her heart, how they looked so sharply in contrast so perfectly suited. Justin's arm slid protectively around his fiancée and they held each other close as they danced,

"Want to dance?" Bill asked, edging his chair closer. Roberta, doing her best to smile, quickly shook her head no. "Thanks, Bill, but I — I really don't feel up to it. The fact is I've suddenly got a splitting headache and I'm feeling dreadfully tired."

"You and me both," Bill said. "Why don't we split?"

After a very brief hesitation, Roberta murmured, "Yes, why don't we?" Surely she would feel somewhat better once she no longer had to exert so much effort not to look Justin's way.

They excused themselves to Justin and Alicia and soon were in a taxi rolling through the night toward their rooms at the Hilton. But after they'd arrived, Bill caught hold of Roberta's arm as she started inside.

"Roberta, hold on just a minute, will you? I know we both agreed that we're tired, and you have a headache besides, but I'd very much like to talk to you, just for a few minutes, please. If we went for a walk along the beach — well, that might even help your headache, mightn't it?"

Roberta hesitated, then agreed. She really wasn't all that anxious to go up to her empty room.

They left the hotel grounds, went down the stone steps onto the sand, and began walking along the beach, a beach that in the bright light of day was one of the most beautiful Roberta had ever seen. Now it was even more beautiful, with the white-crested surf rolling endlessly onto the smooth white sand, then, with a muted hissing sound, withdrawing again, only to come crashing in once more.

After they'd walked for a time, Bill reached across and took her hands. The feel of his thin, nervous fingers was comforting in a way and Roberta, after a moment, gave his hand a warm, friendly squeeze. Bill stopped walking and swung to face her.

"Roberta, the reason I asked you to go for this walk — I said I wanted to talk to you, remember? Well, what I wanted to say . . . I'm not going to find it easy to say this but it's something I've wanted to say for several days now. Once this job is over, Justin's all set to marry Alicia, as you know, as both of us know, and . . . "

Bill stopped, nervously wiping his brow with his handkerchief, then he suddenly blurted out, "So why don't we get married then too? I really like you, Roberta; in these past few weeks I've gotten to know and respect you more than any woman I've ever known, only it — it's even more than that; I've fallen in love with you, so that's why I'm asking you: will you marry me, please?"

Without waiting for an answer, without giving her any chance to speak, Bill stepped forward and pulled her awkwardly into his arms, and bending down pressed his mouth on hers, while hot tears of loneliness . . . frustration . . . pain . . . flooded into Roberta's eyes.

The first proposal of marriage she'd ever received — and she *did* like Bill, she really did.

After the kiss, as Bill pulled her even closer, Roberta found herself going almost limp against him, allowing herself to feel comforted by his nearness. When their three-month assignment was over, she could get married — just as Justin was getting married — if she decided she wanted to.

5

IT had been a truly lovely day, in many ways the nicest they'd yet spent in Jamaica. The Christmas holiday over, the painful hours spent in Alicia's company in Ocho Rios nothing more than a lingering memory, they were now back at work, no longer on the banks of the Rio Grande but along a spectacular stretch of beach along the north coast, as yet undiscovered by tourists and completely unspoiled in its natural beauty. Where bathing and swimming in the Rio Grande had been a continual delight, now sporting in the warm waters of the sparkling Caribbean Sea was an even greater pleasure. Never before had Roberta lived and worked in such a peaceful spot; she felt transported back in time to what it must have been like when the world was gift-wrapped new. And what a lovely world it was!

From dawn until dusk they worked again on their digs gathering tree, earth, sand, water, and air samples to ship for analysis to the Miami lab. Often it rained as they worked, but usually it was such a refreshingly soft rain and rarely did it interfere with what they were doing. If it was raining at night, they journeyed to an abandoned hut they had found, some five hundred yards from the beach, where they could bed down on the wooden slats under the makeshift roof. There were two small rooms, so Roberta had one room to herself while the two men shared the other. And with everyday that passed Roberta felt more at peace with the earth, with her body, and with her heart.

There had been a slight problem their first night there, nothing significant; yet it had threatened, for a day, to pull them apart with strain. After their return to Kingston Christmas night, Justin had told them the following morning that they were going to start work on the north shore. They had packed and left the hotel, driving their little green car. Justin had driven along the shore until he found a spot to suit him; they had unpacked their gear, scouted the area, discovered the sagging two-room shack, and Roberta and Bill had spent a couple of happy hours sweeping it out with palm leaves, dusting the rough boards of the walls and washing them down, with Bill continually teasing her that they were now getting ready to settle down into their first home together.

By evening both were in a highly excitable, festive mood. The shack had a sagging front porch and they gathered there together, all three of them, to feast on their evening meal, and then, while Justin studied his endless reports and papers, she and Bill had gone for a walk along the beach, listening to the eternal rolling in of the sea.

As they walked Bill held her hand and that was nice; as it drew dark he pulled her close and kissed her, a sweet friendly kiss on the mouth. After one kiss Roberta drew back, not wanting any further signs of affection, and hand in hand they strolled back along the beach, in time returning to the shack to crawl into their sleeping bags for the night. By then it had started to rain.

Roberta fell easily to sleep almost as soon as she'd climbed into her bag, off by herself in her private room. Ever since coming to Jamaica, she had not only had a huge appetite, but she had also slept more deeply and refreshingly than ever before, and for the most part she rarely dreamed, though repeatedly she woke with a wonderful feeling of excited anticipation — of what? Of another day spent with Justin and Bill? She really didn't know; she only knew she felt happier than she'd ever felt before. Each day was a treasure to store forever in memory. She wouldn't let herself face that the life she knew now would ever draw to an end.

But of course it would, she knew

that; all the more reason to exult in and fill to bursting every single moment she was given, she told herself. And never, ever let herself think of the fact that one day soon it would all end, and Justin would fly off to marry his love and she would — or wouldn't? — marry Bill. That day would come, of course, but why spoil things by brooding about it? For the most part she didn't. She just enjoyed.

Their first night here, after she and Bill had taken their walk and returned to go to bed, she had fallen to sleep almost immediately, but sometime later had been suddenly startled awake by the feeling — confused and vague to start with as her eyes popped open — that something, or someone, was close to her, breathing on her; she was not alone anymore. The rain had thickened; she could hear it beating down on the sagging roof overhead, could hear it splashing through the various holes, running down the walls. In her sleeping bag she felt warm, dry, snug, and she didn't feel really frightened, but still . . . And then she heard the voice, Bill's voice, and knew that he was the intruder in her room

"Hey, Roberta," Bill's voice whispered, a shrill little whisper as she suddenly felt his hand on her arm. "I hope you weren't sleeping yet but I wanted — "

Another sound intruded, Justin's voice, clipped and furious, a few feet away: "Bill, what the hell do your think you're doing? Get the hell out of there and back out here where you belong!"

There was a flash of lightning and Roberta could see, for an instant, Bill's face as he swung around, still crouched down beside her. "But I was only — "

"I don't give a damn! Get out here right now!"

"But — "

"No buts, damn it!" In the next instant Justin had leaped furiously forward — another lightning flash lit up the room — grabbed Bill's arm and unceremoniously yanked him to his feet, pulling him forcefully out of the room.

Then it was all over, no more sounds apart from the rain beating down overhead, spilling through the numerous holes in the roof. With a sigh Roberta shifted her position, feeling disturbed. She rested her head on one arm and lay awake for some time staring out into the hot blackness of the room. Of course in a way Justin was right, but at the same time his reaction seemed uncalled for.

Bill had looked so upset, so humiliated, like a small boy unjustly accused of a crime he wouldn't think of committing, and after all, Roberta thought, I'm a grown woman, in no way defenseless. Besides which she knew Bill Coffer, trusted him, and was in no way afraid of him, so did Justin have the right to interfere?

In time she finally fell back asleep but she still felt unsure, disturbed, not in the least certain how she felt about what had happened, whose side she was on or if she had to take sides at all. But Bill had looked so dreadfully upset, so outraged, so vulnerable.

In the morning Bill wouldn't speak to Justin at all and spoke to Roberta only in sullen monosyllables, as though what had happened was partially her fault too. As they ate breakfast sitting on the sagging porch of their hut, Roberta kept glancing his way, hoping to catch his eye, to get him back into a better humor. But the few times Bill glanced her way, his eyes darting over, then quickly fleeing again, he didn't seem to gain comfort; instead he seemed to sink even deeper into gloom. For his part, Justin acted his usual self, brisk and cheerful, issuing directions, planning their day, entirely ignoring Bill's sullen unwillingness to speak to him or even look his way. It was as though, for Justin, no problem existed, as he hadn't the least intention, apparently, of acknowledging one.

As they worked that day, Roberta began slowly to be infected by much the same gloom that was eating away at Bill. Justin *had* been wrong, she decided, beginning to feel angry about it; he *had* acted the petty little dictator when he'd had no right to. Who did he think he was, anyway? His right to give Bill and her orders during the day, to organize and direct their work activities she didn't question, but that didn't mean he could order them about during their leisure hours too! She and Bill had spent a warmly friendly afternoon together cleaning out the shack, moving their few possessions in, and after dinner they had gone for a leisurely walk and had felt even closer and friendlier. So what if Bill had thought of something he wanted to say to her that he couldn't wait until morning to say? Was that any of Justin's business? And to yell at Bill like that, to grab him up and humiliate him was surely out of line.

Justin was simply too arrogant and bossy. Well, damn it, she was angry too, just as Bill was. Maybe if the two of them stood loyally by each other, faced Justin together . . . With a tiny leap of her pulse, Roberta knew that that was what she wanted to do.

Early in the afternoon, with Bill still scarcely speaking to her, acknowledging her presence only by an occasional sullen glare in her direction, Roberta approached him and told him she wanted to speak to him.

"Really, Bill," she said softly, well out of the range of Justin's hearing. "I can't see why you should be acting this way with me. I'm on your side in the whole episode; I can quite understand why you're furious at Justin. I'm furious at him too. He seems to think he should be absolute dictator over everything we do, every word we say, and at the moment I'm as sick of it as you are. But why hold it against me?"

Bill stood staring down at her, then suddenly a wide grin broke across his attractive freckled face. "Really?" he said, delight bubbling into his voice. "You don't blame *me* for what happened, you blame *him*? Hey, that's great! I figured you were as upset with me as he was. Roberta, I'm so glad, so relieved!" Bill ended, momentarily putting his hand to her arm, grinning even more broadly.

For the rest of that afternoon they worked together in the warmest harmony, with greater friendliness than ever before. Repeatedly Bill's eyes caught Roberta's and he'd smile, and again Roberta faced how deeply, genuinely fond of him she was. But did that mean she wanted to marry him?

As they ate their evening meal, sitting on the white sand facing the ocean, Bill's face, Roberta noticed, began again to close up, to look sullen and upset. He ate listlessly, staring out at the ocean; then his eyes would circle back, move to Justin, move quickly away again, while Justin again, as in the morning, arrogantly ignored any possible tension existing among the three of them. His thinking seemed to be, Roberta thought in instant anger, that if one ignored something it didn't exist. Within moments she was so filled with rage at him that she wished she had the physical strength to confront him, to grab *his* arm and yank him up and away as he'd done to poor Bill the night before. Who did he think he was, anyway?

Then suddenly the strained silence was broken by Bill, who turned to face Justin, nervously blinking his eyes.

"Mr. Martin, I want to say — " he paused, coughing, then started again, "I mean, Justin, there's something I want to say. About last night — well, I finally see how right you were. When we're off in the wilds like this — I've seen the point made in movies over and over again — it becomes more important than ever to observe the proprieties. If people don't, then everything just goes to pot. So last night I was one hundred percent in the wrong, I see that now, and you were entirely in the right, so I want to apologize to you, and to Roberta too. Also I want to give you both my word that it will never happen again."

"Forget it," Justin said, with his broad irresistible grin. "No big deal. And I overreacted a bit, I'm afraid, for which I apologize." He glanced around at Roberta, still smiling, his eyes warmly drawing her in.

That instant Roberta could feel the anger flow out of her. Would she never learn how to resist this man? A simple smile from him seemed to melt her heart.

The following day, as though in relief to have friendly relations reestablished, everyone seemed in an exuberantly good mood and no day had passed so pleasantly. They quit work rather early, spent time jumping and riding the waves, and then after dinner Bill got out his tape player and put on a tape of Calypso songs he had recorded in Ocho Rios. On the spur of the moment, with bubbling good spirits, Bill and Roberta decided to set up a bamboo pole to work on learning to do the limbo dance

"Bet I can beat you at it," Bill said, in a spurt of uncharacteristic self-confidence as they worked at tying supporting rods onto two poles.

"And what makes you think that?" Roberta countered, tying a knot.

"Because," Bill explained, "you saw what happened in Ocho Rios. The two limbo dancers there were both males, and Justin beat out both those young women. It must have something to do with the difference between the male and female bodies. Males must have an easier time of it."

"Nonsense!" Roberta responded. "In the Limbo Room at the Hilton the girls did every bit as well as the men. Remember that one girl — the one who wore all the bracelets and rings — why, she was the very best one there!"

"The exception that proves the rule," Bill said, laughing. "Want to bet or not?"

"You're on!" Roberta agreed, laughing too.

Soon they had their supporting poles ready to plant in the sand and, after discussion, decided to make it easy on themselves to start with until they caught on to the trick of the thing; therefore, they placed the cross pole at a level barely below Roberta's shoulders. With the beat of the recorded Calypso music on Bill's tape player blaring out at them, they took off their shoes and socks, and, dressed in khaki shorts and T-shirts, plunged into learning the limbo.

They each made it under the first height and readjusted the supporting poles to where the cross pole was a few inches lower. This time they both knocked if off, Bill as he approached it, Roberta just before she would have cleared it. Laughing, they replaced the pole and tried again; this time each one made it under.

"So let's give ourselves a real challenge this time," Roberta suggested, as they again set about adjusting their supporting poles. "Let's go down to about here." She indicated a height about the level of her hip bones.

"For Pete's sake, no!" Bill objected. "Neither one of us will ever make that. Why, we both had to try twice even to make this last height. Going down an inch or two is enough."

Roberta considered arguing some more, then with a smile shrugged it off and they did as Bill wanted, lowering the pole only a couple of inches.

They were working to make it under this height when they both noticed Justin stridng down the beach toward them, smiling.

"That looks like fun," Justin said as he reached them. "Mind if I join you?"

Her pulse instantly pounding happily, Roberta said at once, "Oh, please do." Except in Ocho Rios with his fiancée, Justin had never joined them in their leisure-hour entertainments before.

"Sure, Mr. Martin, if you like," Bill said suddenly, nervously, wiping his arm across his perspiring brow. He walked to his tape player sitting on a palm leaf on the sand, turning the volume down a bit, then muttered half to himself, "Well, that settles who's going to win, all right."

Hearing this, Justin glanced quickly around at Bill, then his eyes circled momentarily to Roberta's face as his cheeks flushed lightly.

"I'm sorry," he said. "Clearly I'm intruding. And I didn't mean I wanted to join the activity, only that I'd like to watch, if you wouldn't mind."

"Oh, feel free to join in, by all means," Bill said in a falsely hearty tone.

"It wouldn't be any fun just watching," Roberta protested, feeling immediately disappointed. "Come on." She laughed briefly, nervously. "In the first place, I know we could both learn an awful lot just from watching you, and, believe me, we need all the help we can get!" She glanced over toward Bill, her eyes asking that he second her in this, that he be happy to have Justin join them instead of looking so mournfully begrudging, but Justin waved her words aside and walked over to stand by one of the supporting poles.

"Well, I'll be happy to watch and give you any pointers I can," he said. "Not that I know the least thing about it, but sometimes an observant bystander can spot a problem that a participant can possibly miss."

The contest continued with Justin watching, but somehow all the fun had gone out of it. Where before there had been constant good-natured kidding between them, now Bill settled down glumly to try to do well, and in consequence, tensing all over, did even more poorly, Roberta doing scarcely any better. Both were too keenly aware that the pole they were trying to wiggle under was inches higher than the one Justin had successfully maneuvered himself under in the nightclub in Ocho Rios.

In time, both Roberta and Bill

managed to make it under at the height they'd set it at, and Justin worked to lower one supporting fork while Roberta and Bill together lowered the other.

Bill gave the new height one long judicious look and said he was retiring before he made a bigger fool of himself than he had already.

"Aw, come on, Bill, at least give it a try," Roberta urged, but Bill just shook his head, scowling and saying he had already strained muscles he didn't even know he had and had had enough.

"But if you don't keep trying, then I'll win the bet," Roberta said.

"That you will," Bill agreed, and strode over to start his tape player up again, which had come to the end of the reel.

Roberta, watching Bill walk off, half decided to give up too, but then she caught the look on Justin's face.

"Come on, give it a try," he said softly. "I know you can make it if you try." Roberta couldn't resist the dare.

Three times in a row, concentrating as hard as she could, doubling over to where she felt she would topple over backwards she failed to make it; each time she knocked against the pole before she was halfway under. Bill stood silently watching, a tiny smile playing around his mouth, while Justin repeatedly talked to her, giving directions, urging her on. Finally, as though wholly caught up in the spirit of it, Justin took two strides forward to reach her, placing one hand on her calf, the other on her shoulder, and began giving her even more explicit advice as he gently pressed her further down.

"The one thing I learned while I was trying it," Justin said, "was not to worry about my head until the very last minute. That's the way most of those professionals did it. Worry about getting your body under, watching yourself as you go, willing yourself down, then only at the very last second drop your head so it will clear too. Come on, I know you can make it if you try."

One last time Roberta tried, and this time she managed to make it under with not even an eighth of an inch to spare.

"That a girl!" Justin exclaimed, grinning, and rushed over to give her a quick congratulatory hug.

"Well, you did it," Bill said, shaking his head in disbelief as he walked over to shake her hand.

When Justin asked if she wanted to lower the pole even farther and try again, Roberta shook her head, laughing. "No, no, enough's enough!" Justin, grinning, answered, "I know what you mean."

In a strangely companionable silence the three of them walked back along the beach toward where their possessions were.

It was a lovely, clear night so they agreed they'd bring their sleeping bags out and sleep on the beach. As she settled down into her bag sometime later, about twenty feet from where the two men were, Roberta found she felt too keyed up to sleep; over and over she kept reliving in her mind the moment when Justin grinning, had hurried over to throw his arm around her shoulders for a brief, friendly hug.

When Bill had proposed marriage to her a few nights before — was it really only a week before? — as they walked along the beach in Ocho Rios, she had at first told him no, in as non-hurtful a way as she knew how, telling him that she didn't feel she knew him well enough to even think about marriage; also she wasn't sure she felt ready yet to settle down into marriage with anyone. Bill had listened as though expecting just those words, but then had responded earnestly that he wished she would at least think it over, saying she didn't have to give him a final answer yet, and they'd left it at that. And in all truth she *was* thinking it over, a great deal.

But — loving Justin as much as she did, how could she even consider marrying anyone else?

Because, Roberta told herself in her more thoughtful moments, she could not have Justin, and therefore her choices were either never to marry or to marry some man other than Justin. It was really as simple as that: no marriage at all or marriage to some other man. And was there any strong reason that that other man shouldn't be Bill? She had liked him at first meeting and since then had grown steadily fonder of him; she felt comfortable and happy with him; they got along beautifully. So . . .

Again, lying in her sleeping bag, staring up at the incredibly dark sky with the brilliantly piercing stars, Roberta relived the moment in which Justin had strode hurriedly to her, putting his arm around her for a quick, pleased hug, and again she shivered with the memory of it, the intense pleasure of it. She just couldn't quite give up hope.

Suddenly Roberta rolled over in her sleeping bag, onto her side, and

188

in despair closed her eyes. Twenty minutes later she rolled over onto her back again, ten minutes later abruptly reopened her eyes. It was no use; she couldn't sleep. She was more wide awake now than when she'd bedded down, which must have been almost an hour before. With a sudden deep sigh. Roberta reached out to unzip her bag, and pulling her legs up she climbed out.

She sat for a moment or two, her chin in her hands, and then decided that exercise might help. Going for a walk might loosen her up and help her relax. Of course the one thing she mustn't do — especially after the fuss of the night before last — was accidentally wander anywhere near where the two men were sleeping. Imagine Justin's fury if he caught her approaching Bill in the middle of the night, as Bill had approached her! Stifling a laugh Roberta began ambling slowly toward the surf. Reaching the wet sand she sat down, propping her chin in her hands.

For quite some time she sat like that, staring out.

Suddenly a voice broke into her thoughts, startling her nearly out of her skin.

"You too?" Justin's voice said. "You can't sleep either?"

"Justin!" Roberta exclaimed, and a brief nervous laugh burst from her. "What are you doing down here?"

"Oh, I often come down here," Justin said, "when I can't sleep, which is about every third night. I get too engrossed in what we're doing, too keyed up. Would you mind if I walked down to join you?" he asked, for he was sitting about ten yards away.

"Of course not," Roberta said.

He walked down to within five feet of her and sat down again, his knees lifted before him, his arms encircling his knees.

They sat for several moments in silence, both gazing out at the surf, the waves cresting and rolling in.

"You know," Roberta said at length,

"it already seems an eternity since Christmas, since we were in Ocho Rios relaxing and enjoying ourselves. Every day here is so busy and so full. I sometimes feel I've lived my whole life right here in Jamaica, working with you and Bill. My life back home seems totally unreal now and so terribly far away."

"I know what you mean," Justin said, and lifting his hands he ran them over his hair.

Roberta allowed herself to circle her eyes around and look directly at him. A moment later Justin seemed to realize it and he glanced around to meet her gaze.

"You must miss Alicia dreadfully," Roberta said. "If our holiday seems as far away to you as it already does to me — "

"Yes," Justin agreed, and sighed.

There was an extended silence again before Roberta murmured on impulse, half to herself, "One reason I couldn't sleep, which doesn't happen often, is

191

that I'm debating a rather crucial decision. While we were in Ocho Rios, Bill proposed, and while I told him no at first, he wants me to think it over. Now I can't think of anything else."

"Marriage, you mean?" Justin asked surprised.

"Yes, of course marriage," Roberta answered, smiling. "Isn't that what a proposal usually is? At first I was sure I didn't want to, but now . . . " her voice trailed off.

"Now you're actually considering it?" Justin demanded, in an even sharper voice. A moment later he stood up, staring down at her, and Roberta found herself climbing up too, to stand facing Justin who stood barely a few feet away. Somehow in standing they seemed to have narrowed the space between them, and also to have put aside some barriers that had existed between them minutes before. Justin's dark eyes, fastened on her, glowed with anger in the dark.

"My God, Roberta, I can't believe it!" Justin exclaimed. "I absolutely cannot believe what I've just heard. Granted that Bill is a very likeable and maybe even physically attractive man — a very physically attractive man — still he — well, he lacks something, can't you see that, something in the way of pride or self-respect? Faced with a challenge, he doesn't gather himself together and give it all he's got; he falls apart. That time he tried to climb the tree — or even tonight. We don't have to go any farther back than tonight. Even in fun he can't bring himself to really try; he gives up in defeat before he even tries. Surely you can see that about him."

Justin, still staring at her, took a quick step toward her and added, "For God's sake, Roberta, I can't believe what you've just said. Can't you see even yet that Bill's simply not like you and me?"

The next moment, so quickly that Roberta could scarcely catch her breath, Justin had taken another long step toward her; his hands grabbed her shoulders and he pulled her to him and kissed her, his mouth pressing forcibly down on hers. Astonished, Roberta couldn't believe it, couldn't believe it was happening. Justin's hands holding her, his mouth angrily claiming hers — and then the next moment it wasn't happening anymore, as quickly as he had grabbed her he released her again, backing away.

"Sorry," Justin muttered, his eyes avoiding hers. "I can't imagine what got into me and, truly, I'm terribly sorry. I had absolutely no business saying a word; certainly I had no business doing what I just did." He ran both hands nervously over his hair, took a step away, then glanced back to face her, saying, "And I give you my word, for whatever it's worth, that I won't act so badly again, butting into your personal life or — making any kind of advance. I only hope you'll be able to forgive and forget."

With this, Justin spun around and began striding rapidly away, while

Roberta stood as though transfixed, staring after him.

It couldn't have happened, it absolutely *could not* have! But — unless she was asleep and dreaming — it had. Justin had kissed her!

6

JUSTIN had made a date to meet Alicia in Montego Bay for New Year's Eve, so on the morning of the 31st they gathered their equipment, packed up, and took off back to Kingston. Spirits were high, expressed in excited talk, laughter, and song. Even though Roberta had a sick feeling deep down inside at the thought of seeing Alicia again, she successfully rose above it and came very close to feeling happy and joyful. After all, it was New Year's Eve!

As they sped over the mountain road, a light, refreshing rain began to fall, which somehow further exhilarated them. Bill leaned forward from the back seat to talk, telling his mournful stories with a straight face that was wonderfully comic and amusing.

"I swear, Coffer," Justin said at

one point, having just laughed until tears came to his eyes, "you've missed your calling. Instead of doing this kind of work, you ought to go into entertaining."

Bill's thin freckled face blushed with pleasure. "Oh, no, hardly," he protested, "though it's nice of you to say so. But if there's one thing I know it's my limitations, and having to get up in front of a crowd would absolutely paralyze me. I wouldn't be able to talk coherently at all."

"Which might make your stories even funnier," Roberta suggested, glancing around to smile at him, sharply reminded of Justin's perceptive comments about Bill. Ever since that night — the night Justin had kissed her — he had scarcely even looked her way; he had, in fact, tended to act even more formally with her, more distant than before. As he had said, she should forget about that night, as he surely already had.

"Of course," Justin began a moment later, all suggestion of laughter gone from his face, "knowing one's limitations is good, of course. I suppose one is in serious trouble if no limitations of any kind are faced. But still don't you think, Coffer — well, doesn't it strike you occasionally that the problem with the world is not that people don't know their limitations, but rather that they constantly impose all kinds of artificial limitations on themselves, cheating themselves dreadfully?"

Bill's freckled face blushed even pinker as he tossed his thick red hair back, saying, "How do you mean, sir? I'm not sure I follow you."

"Well," Justin explained, "consider what you've just said, that you know you could never be an entertainer as the mere idea paralyzes you with fright. For almost an hour now you've been entertaining Roberta and me, sending us both into gales of laughter, and apparently that didn't frighten you at all."

"I'm flattered that you enjoyed it," Bill said sounding suddenly ill at ease and tense. "But that's an entirely different thing."

"Why is it entirely different?" Justin snapped back. "If you can entertain two people, why not three? Or four? At what point does fright set in? You say you know your limitations, but have you ever given it a try? Have you ever properly tested your talent to see exactly how far it will stretch? Until you accept the challenge and really test yourself, how can you possibly make the statement that you know your limitations? I would suggest that you don't have the least idea what your limitations are. All you know at this point are your fears, which you foolishly allow to rule you. Which is what I was saying a moment before. Far too many people do the same thing, imposing artificial limitations on themselves which cheat them out of all the fun. What's the point of living if we refuse to accept challenges to find out what we're all about?"

As Justin's clipped voice, just slightly

tinged with anger, stopped, a tense silence fell. The car continued to barrel forward through the light misty rain. Bill sat forward a few moments longer, then muttered an embarrassed, "Yeah, I suppose," and drew back to sit slouched on the back seat. Glancing around at him, Roberta forced a friendly smile. Just a few minutes ago everyone's spirits had been riding high; they'd all been laughing together, feeling festive in keeping with the time of year, and now look! Did Justin always have to make a federal case out of everything? Couldn't he ever accept things — people — as they were, without imposing his own impossible standards on them? As Roberta glanced back at Bill, his eyebrows lifted, then drew back down, and his expression said clearly: 'See? You see what he's like? No matter what I do, I'm in the wrong. I can't even tell a few funny stories that you both laughed at without having to listen to a tirade about what a lousy failure I am. I can't win for losing — do you wonder I get tired of trying?'

Sighing, Roberta swung around again, glancing momentarily at Justin, who sat upright, almost stiff, behind the wheel. The rain, growing heavier, splashed down on the windshield, running down in little rivulets, and Justin switched the wipers on to a higher sped.

Suddenly he broke the silence, turning partly around to face the back seat.

"Hey, Bill, I'm sorry. I don't know what gets into me to sound off like that. Maybe I'm a frustrated preacher; do you suppose that's it?" His face broke into a wide apologetic grin; and as he glanced forward again, his eyes momentarily caught Roberta's, asking her forgiveness too, and Roberta, in spite of herself, felt her insides flip. How could you stay angry long at a man like that? Again she remembered — as she had a hundred times before — that Justin had kissed her, had actually drawn her into his arms and kissed her, and her heart threatened to burst, both with excitement and pain. So he'd kissed her once — that didn't mean he ever would again. In fact, she knew perfectly well it never *would* happen again.

Sighing, Roberta turned to stare forlornly out the window, hearing Bill mutter in answer to Justin, "The thing is, Mr. Martin, you're probably right, which means there's no need to apologize," following which, silence again fell on the car.

Arriving at the hotel in Kingston, they unpacked the car and went to their separate rooms to bathe and change clothes, Roberta trying to decide whether she preferred to fly off to Montego Bay with Justin — to be joined by Alicia — or to stay behind in Kingston to spend a quiet evening here with Bill. Bill had said unwaveringly from the first that he would stay or go depending on what Roberta decided to do.

On the one hand, it hurt to pass up any time she might spend with

Justin, especially a holiday; but on the other, to spend another evening in Alicia Markham's company was not something she looked forward to.

As she lay soaking in a warm soapy tub, Roberta tried to decide. New Year's Eve. At midnight — well, at midnight wasn't it customary to kiss whoever was nearby, not just the one person you were with but anyone you knew well or cared about? Once this assignment was over and she returned home, all she'd have to keep her company would be her memories. Should she forego what might be the loveliest memory of all simply because there'd be pain mixed with it? A bittersweet memory — wasn't that better than no memory at all?

As she climbed out of the tub at last and began drying off, Roberta still hadn't really made up her mind. She heard the phone ringing, abruptly became aware that it had been ringing for quite some time, and, wrapping herself in the bath towel, walked out to answer it.

Justin's voice said, very cheerfully, "Well, where have you been? I'd about decided you'd drowned. I checked with the airport and we're cleared for take off in thirty minutes. Are you and Bill going along or not?"

"Well — " In spite of her best efforts to remain calm and detached, Roberta's heart began to pound and the sick feeling she'd been fighting down all day sprouted into full-fledged nausea. "Well, I . . . Darn it, Justin, I just can't decide!"

"There are two sides to it, all right," Justin said in the same cheerful voice. "According to the weather reports the rain farther north is even heavier than here. If we delay at all in taking off, we might lose clearance, which is why I don't want to fool around. On the one hand I'd be glad for the company — you and Bill are my friends, no matter how I act sometimes — but on the other hand it's obvious you'll be safer and drier if you stay right here. So I'm not urging you to come; in fact I rather think you'll be better off if you don't, but I didn't want to go off and leave you if you're of a strong mind to go."

"I'm of a strong mind to go!" Roberta announced firmly in answer, that moment making up her mind. If Justin was going to go flying off when it wasn't safe, then she wanted to be with him.

"Are you sure?" Justin countered, sounding both surprised and upset. "I honestly think you should reconsider and stay right here. In fact, damn it, I shouldn't even have phoned you. I should have just gone off on my own. It's one thing to possibly risk my own neck, but to drag along two people I care about — "

"You aren't dragging us along, Justin, we are going of our own free will, and as you said before, nothing in life is guaranteed. I'm sure we'll be fine."

After a brief silence Justin said,

"Well, all right. I'll meet both of you down in the lobby as fast as you can make it."

"Right," Roberta agreed, feeling suddenly elated and excited. Obviously I'm out of my mind, completely out of my mind, she conceded, hurriedly drying and dressing, yet she didn't feel crazy. She felt wide awake, alert, sure of what she was doing and why she wanted to do it. Surely Justin would be in somewhat less danger if she and Bill were there to — well, just to be there, if nothing else. To keep him company, to offer assistance if an emergency arose. Shivering, Roberta refused to give further thought to this possibility; of course they would be all right, all three of them!

She phoned Bill, told him she'd decided to go and suggested that he needn't go along unless he truly wanted to; but he insisted again that if she planned to go, he was going, too.

"Then we're meeting Justin downstairs as soon as possible," Roberta said and, laughing again, hung up the phone. New Year's Eve, the most exciting night of the year during this, the most exciting time of her life!

In less than thirty minutes they were at the airport, climbing into the small plane, and Justin was settling down in front of the controls and getting ready for take off.

Bill, sitting alongside Roberta in the passenger seats, looked scared, Roberta thought. Momentarily she felt a pang of guilt for deciding to take this flight, knowing that it meant Bill would go, too. To reassure herself as much as to comfort him, she reached over to press her hand on his.

"Don't worry, we'll make it all right," she murmured softly, hoping Justin wouldn't hear.

Bill's eyes jerked up and swung around to challenge hers. "Oh, I'm sure we will. There's no question of that, is there? I mean — surely a little rain is no big problem, is it? Planes fly in heavier rain than this all the time."

"Right, of course they do," Roberta agreed.

Justin glanced around, grinning, and Roberta smiled back.

"All set," Justin said, and pulling out the throttle he switched on the engine, causing the light plane to shudder and shake. Then it was rolling forward, leaving the ground, and they were up in the air. Roberta laughed excitedly, telling herself again that she must be crazy.

Her good spirits seemed to communicate to Bill and before long he was relaxing and laughing too. They began to sing, Christmas songs for the most part, and just as it occurred to Roberta that perhaps they should ask Justin, who sat just before them in the pilot's seat, if the singing was bothering him, she became aware that Justin was joining in, singing with them. She was ecstatic!

After they'd finished their fourth version of 'Auld Lang Syne,' Justin glanced around, shouting over the noise of the engine, "How about

'Embraceable You,' do you happen to know that? It's an old song, I know, but maybe you know it?"

"Of course," Roberta yelled back. It was all too clear whom Justin was thinking about: Alicia, the woman he loved, his sweet 'embraceable' one. Turning to smile at Bill, Roberta broke into the opening words of the song, Bill joined in, and, although it was difficult to hear his voice over the roar of the engine, Roberta could see that Justin was singing too. Singing to, singing of Alicia, flying off to see her no matter the weather, no matter the risk. If only some man would love me that much, Roberta sighed.

The moment she thought this, Roberta felt a second wave of guilt. Sitting right here beside her, his long thin freckled face still a little pale, sat a man who *did* love her that much, who had insisted that if she planned to make this trip, he would not under any circumstances stay behind. Just because the man who loved her wasn't the man she loved . . .

Exasperated, Roberta thought: Justin loves Alicia, I love Justin but Bill loves me. Is this always the way of the world? She could feel herself becoming painfully sentimental as Bill broke into another song, 'Sentimental Journey.' *Going to take a sentimental journey* . . .

They were crooning a soft rendition of 'Silent Night,' trying to harmonize, when the plane first took a sharp dip, dropping so sharply that they all seemed to lift up from their seats, only to be slammed back down. Behind the controls, Justin muttered, "Damn!" Then rapidly worked a couple of levers and the plane seemed to level off and fly smoothly again.

"Anything the matter?" Roberta called to him, after telling herself that she shouldn't bother him.

Justin glanced back, answering, "No, no problem," but nevertheless the singing died away, everyone's attention suddenly returning to the flight.

Wiping mist off her window and peering out, Roberta saw that, though it wasn't yet six o'clock, it seemed pitch black. Rain pelted against the window, a hard slashing rain much heavier than before. Suddenly there was a lightning flash, so close it seemed almost to hit the right wing, followed almost at once by a deafening clap of thunder. The plane dropped sharply a second time. Struggling to get the plane to level off again, Justin muttered a string of expletives under his breath.

Bill hunched forward, staring out the small window on his side of the plane. After a moment he turned to look at Roberta, then reached out and took her hand, his face now even more noticeably green.

"I just want you to know," he said mournfully, "I've really enjoyed working with you, getting to know you. It was the greatest experience of my life."

Roberta, in annoyance, jerked her hand back. "Oh, come on, Bill, knock it off!" she snapped. "Just because it's raining a bit — "

"Raining a bit!" Bill exclaimed. "That's a thunderstorm out there, a storm that can easily toss this plane around and break it in two as you or I could snap off a matchstick. Face it, Roberta, we're in for it now."

As though to confirm his pessimistic words, the plane dropped again, even more sharply, and seemed to swerve out of control. Working with the controls, Justin swore again, somewhat more loudly.

"Bill, Roberta, one of you," he yelled a moment later, over the sputtering noise of the engine and the furious blasting noise of the storm, "one of you come up here, please. Right now, please!"

In an instant Roberta was on her feet, moving forward, wiggling into the co-pilot's seat. Justin glanced momentarily around, as though scarcely taking in who it was who had joined him, just grateful to have someone there.

"Grab this with both hands," Justin instructed her, "and do your damndest to hold on."

"That's it?" Roberta asked, following his instructions.

"That's it. But it's awful damn important, so don't let go."

"Right." She began exerting all her strength to hold the control as steady as she was able to.

Up front, through the windshield, the sky seemed a thick sheet of rain. One lightning flash followed another now, with scarcely a moment's intermission; thunder clapped and rocked the plane, causing it to drop, swerve, tip perilously to the right. Justin continued to work furiously at the controls, perspiration now beading on his brow, running down the sides of his face.

"We — we are going to make it through, aren't we?" Roberta dared to ask after a time, fastening her eyes on Justin's profile, on the face she so loved to watch. Fully expecting Justin to say that of course they were, she was terribly jarred to hear him mutter,

"No, I'm afraid not. No way, no way."

Really? she wanted to say, but she couldn't quite get herself together enough to say it. Her mouth felt suddenly horribly dry; she felt a funny excitement in the pit of her stomach; she wondered how the end would come. Would the plane break apart? Crash down? Or would lightning hit them and kill them right here where they sat? She felt terribly curious, wanting to ask Justin what he meant, what kind of disaster he saw for them, but she still couldn't seem to speak. All she seemed able to do was to sit there, furiously struggling to hold the control Justin had turned over to her, watching his face, aching to say to him the very same things that Bill had said to her a few minutes before, that working with him, getting to know him, had been the greatest experience of her life. But she couldn't seem to get the words out, and surely Justin wouldn't have any great interest in hearing them anyway. Her feelings right now were certainly the least of his problems.

"Damn it anyway," Justin said, a small tense smile pulling around his mouth, "I hate like hell to turn back, but you can see for yourself we simply have no choice. There's no way of telling how far north or east this storm front extends, or how much worse it might get. If I were up here alone I might risk it, though I probably wouldn't even then. No matter how I feel about it, we have to turn back."

Roberta flashed out an answering sympathetic smile, relief flooding through her. So that's what he'd meant — they weren't going to make it through to Montego Bay, not that they weren't going to make it safely down! She didn't have to spend the evening watching Justin with Alicia after all; rather, once Justin had turned them back around, she and Bill would have him all to themselves back in Kingston. It seemed that luck was with her after all.

After a time Justin brought the plane under sufficient control to swing it around; instead of heading into the storm they hastily flew away from it, and almost before it seemed possible, they were bouncing down onto the runway at the Kingston airport.

As soon as they had safely landed and disembarked from the plane, Bill ran off to find a taxi.

"I'll have to phone Alicia the moment we reach the hotel," Justin remarked to Roberta, sounding upset and gloomy. "Which I sure hate to do. I know how much she's been looking forward to tonight, just as I have, and now to have this happen. This is sure one hell of a New Year's Eve!"

Hoping to comfort him, Roberta said, "Well, is there the least chance that Alicia could come over here? I don't mean tonight of course, but if the weather should clear up tomorrow?"

"Afraid not," Justin murmured, lifting

his hands to rub them against his cheeks. "No matter what the weather does, she won't be able to come. She's with her aunt and uncle aboard their yacht, and they're set to leave Montego Bay for Nassau, then on to Miami. They were nice enough to come to Jamaica so we could see each other, but I know they won't delay leaving any longer."

Justin paused momentarily, then added, "You see, Alicia doesn't have any money of her own. She lives with her aunt and uncle and is entirely dependent on them, so when they leave Montego Bay, she leaves with them. She has no choice."

And why doesn't she have a choice? Roberta wondered instantly, rather angrily. *If I loved a man* . . . Justin had remarked on Christmas Day in Ocho Rios that he and Alicia had known each other for over three years, which meant that Alicia had had all that time to rearrange her life to spend it with the man she planned to marry.

If she had no particular career interests of her own, why hadn't she prepared herself so that she could assist Justin in *his* work? Why wasn't she on this assignment with him right now? What — apart from her apparent 'addiction' to jet-set life — kept her from bidding farewell to her aunt and uncle this very day and coming to Kingston? If she really loved Justin . . .

Snapping irritably at herself, Roberta told herself she had no business judging another woman's way of loving. No doubt there were numerous considerations about which she knew absolutely nothing, and therefore she couldn't possibly make a fair judgement.

"Roberta — Roberta, there is something I very much want to say to you," Justin began nervously interrupting her thoughts. "And I feel that possibly this is the right time to say it. I've known few people in my life that I can truly say I trusted, people that I knew wouldn't collapse under pressure, that I knew could be counted on in any and every situation; and this is something I very much value in people, the ability to come through in an emergency. Again tonight you've shown you're one of those people: you've got it all together, you don't fall apart, and I want to say — well, I just want to say I admire and respect you very much, and I'm delighted to have you as my friend."

The next moment — as Roberta's insides did a wild excited flip — Justin leaned close and pressed his lips affectionately against her cheek, his hand squeezing her hand as he did so, and Roberta felt happy tears flood her eyes. After the kiss, they stood silently together in the heavy rain, Justin still holding her hand.

Then a taxi pulled up, and it was time for them to head back to the hotel. In the lobby, Justin wished them a Happy New Year and hurried up to his room to phone Alicia.

"But — " Roberta stammered, "but surely you'll meet us later for dinner and to spend the evening?" *New Year's Eve*. Surely he'd be with them when the clock struck midnight, everyone happily welcomed in the New Year, and friends and lovers kissed?

Justin glanced back, smiling, then murmured, "No, no, I don't think so tonight. Thank you anyway, but I'll just have something sent to my room. But you two have a bang-up time. I plan to settle down to study some reports that just came in."

"But you can't!" Roberta protested, tears of frustration threatening to flood her eyes. Weren't the three of them buddies now, hadn't they just risked their lives together in that foolish attempt to keep Justin's date with Alicia, and wasn't this a holiday?

"And why can't I?" Justin countered, his dark eyes flashing with amusement.

"Because it's New Year's Eve!" Roberta exclaimed. "No one works on New Year's Eve!"

"I do," Justin said, turning away again, tossing back over his shoulder, "but you two have a good time," and then he was striding rapidly away and there was nothing Roberta could do but stand staring after him, feeling disappointed. For Alicia he had happily risked his life, so determined had he been to see her, so anxious to spend this holiday evening with her. But for her, Roberta — his good friend Roberta, whom he respected and admired — he wouldn't even postpone reading some of his endless reports!

As she stared after him, hot tears stinging her eyes, Roberta felt a hand touch her arm as Bill remarked softly into her ear, "For whatever it's worth, sweetheart, you still have me."

Swinging her eyes quickly around to his, forcing out a friendly smile, Roberta muttered, "Bill, you're sweet." Which he was.

But how much *was* it worth to have him?

7

FOR the first few days of the new year they remained in Kingston, at the hotel, while Justin dictated a seemingly endless stream of memos and reports, but by the end of the week they were back at work in the field again.

As the days and weeks sped by, it seemed to Roberta that Justin was becoming disturbingly remote, speaking to her less often, rarely even glancing her way. From New Year's Day on she had sensed some change in him and had spent hours each day, while hard at work digging, climbing, or cataloging, trying to figure it out, to put her finger on exactly in what way his behavior toward her had changed, and it seemed to her that she had finally successfully pinpointed it.

Whereas during their first month

together, Justin had seemed friendly enough, and appreciative, it had been in a completely casual, almost absent-minded way, the same way he would have been friendly toward, and appreciative of, a well-programmed functional robot; in fact, truth to tell, he would undoubtedly have preferred such a robot. Never at any time had he seemed to feel any need to put special distance between them; the distance was already there, in a sense built in. Obviously throughout that period he could look at her, talk to her, work alongside her without giving her a single thought as a woman, just as he'd promised he would. But, beginning with the night on the beach when neither of them had been able to sleep and she'd told him about Bill's proposal, after he'd suddenly grabbed her close and to her astonishment kissed her, from that night on she had become something more than a robot to him — or was it something less? That night he had apparently, in spite of his best intentions, begun to see her as a person, even more, as a *female*, and from that moment on their relationship had changed.

In the excitement of the holidays and their planned trip to Montego Bay, she hadn't become immediately aware of it, but from the time Justin had managed to land them safely, albeit a bit roughly, back in Kingston after their frightening flight . . . Well, there was just no doubting it anymore, Roberta thought sadly, from the moment they had disembarked from the plane, the change in their relationship had become increasingly apparent.

Sighing, Roberta pushed off from shore on a small square bamboo raft and began to navigate her way across the shallow river, using a pole to propel the raft. They were on the banks of a different river now, the Black River, in southwest Jamaica. For the past week they had been working their way along the southern coast, had arrived at the mouth of the Black

River the day before, and Justin had said they'd remain in this vicinity for a couple of days.

When Justin had told them that they'd only be staying there a couple of days, Roberta had been pleased, and so had Bill. Somehow, though she'd loved almost every other place they'd worked here in Jamaica, she'd had an adverse reaction at the first sight of this river. Maybe it was just because her spirits were beginning to flag a bit; mostly, she supposed, because she was still having a problem figuring out, and adjusting to, Justin's new attitude toward her.

Nonsense! Roberta scolded herself again; Justin hadn't changed toward her at all! The problem was that, after the night he'd kissed her, even more after their perilous flight and his sweet words following it, she had *expected* him to change toward her, had dared allow herself the fierce hope that he would. Instead he'd stayed the same, which hurt, and it was this hurt that she hadn't yet adjusted to.

Roberta drew up the pole and picked up the broad paddle to use instead. The paddle was made of bamboo leaves stiffened every few inches with bamboo stems lashed on; it seemed to work remarkably well, as did the long pole closer to shore. They had found the raft, with the pole and paddle, pulled up along the shore yesterday afternoon, apparently abandoned by its owner, or at least unclaimed, and had made use of it to take them across the river. Some twenty minutes before, as they worked, Justin had realized he needed a tool he'd left in the car, which was on the far side of the river from where they were, and Roberta, feeling tired and hot, and a bit restless, had offered to take the raft across the river to get the tool.

"You're sure you can handle the raft all right?" Justin had asked, sounding rather tense, not glancing at her. "If you like, take Bill along with you."

"Oh, no, I can handle it fine by myself," Roberta had answered quickly, not wanting, at that particular moment, to have Bill along. In the mood she was in, more than anything else she wanted time alone.

She'd gotten across the river without the least problem, as she'd known she would, had walked to the car, gotten the tool — which was small enough to fit into her shirt pocket — and was on her way back, still in the same agitated, somewhat depressed mood. What was the matter with her that she couldn't enjoy the days — and the lovely nights — anymore?

Frowning, sighing again, she knelt on the raft and stopped paddling momentarily, allowing the raft to drift. There was little current at the moment in the sluggish, muddy river, and even if she didn't paddle for some time she wouldn't drift far. Roberta let go of the bamboo paddle and used both hands to push back her hair. For almost all of the time they'd been in Jamaica she had tied back her long thick hair at the start of each workday; it seemed a necessity to do so, to get it out of the way. Yet today, for some reason, in rebellion against something, she hadn't tied it back, only to be rewarded by a brief puzzled look from both Justin and Bill when they saw her like that, her long dark hair framing her face. And a momentary look of puzzlement on their faces was remarkably little reward considering the irritating problem her free hair posed with every move she made.

So I'll tie it back again the moment I reach shore, Roberta decided, feeling angry at herself for the mood she was in.

Defiantly, Roberta sank the paddle over the side of the raft, into the river and in surprise felt it snap off. Lifting what was left out of the water, she saw that half of the paddle was gone. She glanced over the side of the raft — and that moment her heart seemed to stop absolutely dead, as the greatest panic of her life shot through her. *A crocodile!*

As she stared in terror, Roberta

stiffled an outcry, pressing her free hand to her mouth, and for a moment she felt so paralyzed with fear she couldn't even breathe. The crocodile, only the very top of its long pointed snout above water, seemed to be drifting with her slowly down the river, almost as though escorting her. Did the beast want the rest of the mangled paddle, was that why he was still so near? Or was it a man-eater after *her*? Oh, if only she had some clearer idea of what crocodiles were like! Did they, like most members of the animal kingdom, attack only when attacked, when threatened? But a crocodile wasn't an animal, it was a reptile, and at least some of them were man-eaters, she was sure of that.

Meanwhile, the raft was drifting, drifting, and the crocodile was still there, its eyes and nose edging out of the water. Had it noticed her? Was it watching her? If she tried to use what was left of the paddle to paddle away, or if she tried to use the pole, what would happen?

Her heart pounding, her mouth and throat so dry she felt hardly able to breathe, Roberta remained as motionless as possible until, to her intense relief, she saw the beast slither off through the water, gliding toward the shore, behind her. Instinctively she drew in a long, deep breath, but then, as she moved her eyes toward the shore she was heading for she froze. There wasn't just the one crocodile. Another had surfaced on her other side!

A second one — and how many more? Had she unknowingly taken her raft right into a school of them? Did crocodiles run in schools? How many were there apt to be? Had they come into the river after her, disturbed by the raft? Would they attack her without provocation? Or was her mere presence here provocation enough?

Oh, God help me! Roberta thought, and in panic lifted her eyes to the far bank. There she saw two motionless figures, Justin and Bill, staring fixedly out at her. Justin stood with one hand over his eyes, staring, his other hand on his hip; Bill had both hands cradled over his eyes and stood half bending over, as though he was fighting nausea — again.

Oh, go ahead and throw up, Bill, why fight it? Roberta thought, and her dry lips all but broke into a smile. So far, apart from cracking off the paddle, the crocodiles had made absolutely no move to attack her. Maybe they were friendly creatures simply out for a mid-morning swim. If she dared to put the paddle over the edge, and paddled very slowly, calmly, moving with great care, what would happen?

The second crocodile, its one visible eye moistly glistening in the sun, edged on past the raft, and Roberta, summoning all the courage she could, gripped the torn-off paddle firmly in hand, took a deep breath, eased the face of the paddle down into the water alongside the raft. At first she felt that the raft wasn't responding at all, was simply continuing its slow drift with the current; but after a second slow pull of the paddle, then a third, the raft seemed to slip a ways toward the shore, and with a bounding leap of hope — neither crocodile seemed to be paying the least attention to her! — Roberta continued to paddle slowly to shore. Justin and Bill had both turned and were striding hurriedly down toward where she was headed; as she got within ten feet of shore, Roberta hurriedly glanced around, but thankfully there was no sign of the crocodile. Grabbing up the long pole with trembling hands, she got up onto shaky legs and pushed the pole down into the riverbed, which sent the raft scurrying toward shore. Three more pushes and she was stepping off the raft, a shaky bundle of quivering nerves and relief.

"Roberta, good girl!" Justin cried, and the next moment his arms were about her, pulling her close. For several moments he held her like that, pressed close against him, his heart seeming to beat almost as fast and as hard as hers.

His lips pressed a hard kiss on the side of her face just before his arms loosened and he let her go.

For a moment they stood facing each other, Justin's eyes, full of pain and relief, meeting hers, his hands still gripping her arms, while Roberta grinned helplessly at him, tears rolling down her cheeks.

Only then did the sound of Bill's retching penetrate into Roberta's consciousness. As Justin's hands at last released her arms, Roberta glanced around and saw Bill over at the edge of the river, bent forward, vomiting.

"Poor guy," Justin murmured. "Just can't seem to get his nerves under any kind of control. But if he ever had an excuse for being nervous, he had it today."

"Bill and me both," Roberta said.

"Yes," Justin responded softly, "but you handled the situation to perfection *without* getting sick."

Somehow her fright on the river put everything back into better perspective, and for the rest of that day, and for the days that followed, Roberta did not again fall into the gloomy moodiness she had allowed herself to slip into before. So Justin would never love her; surely she could live with that. She'd known almost from the moment they met that he was in love with someone else, engaged to be married, that there was no hope of her ever winning his love. That didn't mean she couldn't enjoy the companionship they shared, this lovely time working together when she knew him in a way that Alicia didn't and probably never would.

When they returned to their hotel rooms in Kingston at the end of January, there was a message from Alicia that she had flown into Nassau and hoped that Justin would be able to fly over to spend an evening with her.

Justin told them about the message as they were having dinner, not with the excited boyish grin with which he had told them of the first message from Alicia at Christmas — how delighted he had seemed that time! Now as he told them, his face seemed caught in a thoughtful scowl and he certainly did not act terribly pleased.

"Are you going to fly over?" Roberta asked, wondering if there was some reason Justin couldn't go, if that was his reason for looking upset.

"Of course I'm going," Justin responded, with a slight impatient snap to his voice. "I brought it up simply because I want to know whether you and Bill want to go along."

"Oh." Roberta took a bite of her steak, glanced around at Bill, and asked how he felt about it.

His freckled face flushed, Bill shrugged. "I don't care, Roberta, it's entirely up to you. If you want to go, fine, but if you don't that's okay too." His eyes dropped to his plate and he concentrated on eating again.

Roberta ate for a time in silence, then Justin asked, an even more pronounced edge to his voice, "Well, are you two going or not? My plan is to leave sometime late tomorrow afternoon. I've got too much to do to leave tonight; besides which even if we left immediately after dinner it would be close to midnight before we reached Nassau, so it seems senseless to rush off tonight. We're most certainly all entitled to a day or two off, but you can spend your free time here, or take the car anywhere you might want to go, or fly to Nassau with me. Whatever suits you."

Momentarily Justin's eyes met Roberta's, as though challenging her. Then with a shrug he circled his eyes away and lifted his wineglass to sip at his wine.

"Well, I just don't know," Roberta murmured. She remembered the previous trip, the flight to Ocho Rios at Christmas — was it really only a month before? — when Justin had come bursting into her room and had called out to her excitedly to get out of the bath and get ready to leave. That time he had seemed so eager to have her go, as though he'd carry her along by the sheer force of his own will if necessary, while now — well, his voice and expression rather indicated he wished he could go by himself, didn't they? Apparently this time he'd rather not have her and Bill tag along.

"Up to you," Bill muttered again, glancing up, his mouth breaking into a friendly smile.

"Well, I think that this time we'll pass up the trip and just stay here. Personally I think I'd just as soon rest and relax our whole time off."

"Well, as Bill says, it's entirely up to you," Justin snapped, his voice clipped and sharp. He lifted one hand, motioning toward a waiter, then his eyes met Roberta's, an angry look flashing in them.

"But if it's because of that flight we took New Year's Eve, I'd like to mention that I've already checked with the weather bureau and there is no storm in sight for the next few days. We'd be making the flight during daylight hours, not at night, and there's no reason to suppose that anything at all will go wrong. So I hope you won't stay here due to any worry on that score." His dark eyes under the thick black brows, continued to hold hers, flashing angrily at her.

"Oh, it isn't that at all," Roberta responded hastily, her pulse beginning to race. "In fact, that hadn't even crossed my mind. But I really think I'd prefer not to go."

"As you wish," Justin muttered, eyes dropping. The waiter came over with the new bottle of wine Justin had ordered. After he'd filled his own glass, Roberta and Bill having both declined any refill, Justin supped at his wine and then remarked, "Personally, however, I think you're both being extremely foolish. How likely are you ever to return to this part of the globe again? The Paradise Island Casino in Nassau is one of the most famous in the world. Why miss the chance to see it? From what Alicia said, the Casino has a great new floor show so even if you haven't the least interest in gambling, there's no reason not to go to enjoy the show."

"Well," Roberta said nervously putting her knife and fork down and reaching for her still full wineglass, "if you'd really rather we went . . . " Her voice died out.

Justin shrugged, quickly moving his eyes away again. "As I said, it's entirely up to you, do as you please. I just think you should weigh all sides before deciding, that's all." Picking up his glass, he gulped down some wine.

So you just won't — can't — break down and say you'd like us to go, Roberta thought, gazing at his profile as Justin stared off. But — why did he care whether or not they went? Frowning, Roberta thought of Alicia, who certainly would not relish the company. But if Justin really wanted them to go . . .

The question was settled the next morning when Roberta stopped by

Bill's room on her way for breakfast and found him still in bed, suffering alternate chills and fevers.

"You wouldn't believe the night I had," Bill said, his thin face breaking into a feeble grin. "For a time I hallucinated something dreadful, saw you and then myself on the river, crocodiles all over — and, boy, that was only the beginning!" he ended, suddenly caught in such violent shivers that his teeth rattled. His face was abnormally flushed, his skin burning hot to the touch, yet he was heavily bundled up because, he said, he felt so cold.

"You poor thing," Roberta murmured, and went immediately to the phone to call for a doctor.

An hour later the doctor, an Englishman on vacation who just happened to be staying at the hotel, had come and gone. After checking Bill over, the doctor said that in his opinion it was nothing more than a bad case of the flu, complicated by a slight case of sunstroke and brought on, no doubt, by physical and nervous exhaustion. He gave Bill an injection, left some liquid medication, ordered him to rest in bed, eating lightly, until completely over all his symptoms.

At lunch with Justin, Roberta reported on the doctor's findings, while Justin listened with interest and concern.

"So of course this ends any talk of our going to Nassau with you," Roberta ended feeling this scarcely needed to be put into words.

Justin nodded, continued to eat, then a moment later looked up to say, "I don't suppose you'd have any interest in going without him? I mean, after all he'd be perfectly all right here, we could arrange to have someone look in on him or even hire a full-time nurse. What do you say, want to go?"

Roberta's eyes lifted, met Justin's directly. Hours alone in the plane with him, and he must want her to go or he wouldn't be so persistent. Maybe he felt she had been working so hard she truly deserved a couple of days off, a day or two of fun and entertainment, not two days of taking care of an invalid. Surely that was it.

"Thank you, Justin," she murmured at last, "but I really don't think that, under the circumstances, I want to go. I'd really rather stay here."

Justin continued to stare another moment or two, then his eyes lowered and he shrugged. "Whatever you say." Three hours later, when she was up in her room reading and resting, he phoned to tell her he was leaving.

"I trust Bill will be fine by the time I return," he said, "and for Pete's sake don't wear yourself out taking care of him."

Laughing, Roberta answered, "Don't worry, I won't. Say hello to Alicia for Bill and me, and have a truly wonderful time."

"Thank you, I'll try," Justin said, and hung up.

It was three days before Justin returned. By then Bill was up and around again, though still feeling weak. Justin had phoned daily during his absence to inquire as to Bill's state of health, each time ordered Roberta to try to catch up on her rest, and not to knock herself out administering to Bill's needs.

"It's bad enough that one of us should be sick," Justin said. "Let's not make it two. So you take it as easy as you possibly can, Roberta, you hear me?"

"I hear you," Roberta responded, laughing. How like a grouchy old father or a deeply concerned brother Justin sounded over the phone! Whenever she tried to get the conversation away from Bill and herself by asking whether he was having a good time in Nassau, Justin would quickly brush the question aside — "Yes, I'm having a fine time, but — " as though he did not wish her to pry into his personal life.

On the afternoon of his third day away, Justin flew back, making next-to-no comment about Alicia or his trip.

Finding Bill still not completely up to par, Justin insisted that they needed to spend time with the reports they'd gathered so far anyway.

For another week they stayed at the hotel, their days falling into a relatively easy pattern. For two to three hours each moring, and occasionally again in the afternoon, Justin would dictate to Roberta, summarizing the lab analysis work done for them in Miami. While he was studying and digesting further reports, Roberta typed up her notes. Bill rested, went for an occasional brief swim, and in the evenings went for short walks with Roberta.

"I feel like such a weakling," Bill muttered one day to Justin, "such a drag, such a failure," but Justin, with a quick grin, snapped that that was nonsense, he shouldn't feel that way.

"Could have happened to any one of us," Justin insisted. "It could just as easily have been I who got sick, or even Roberta here."

Suddenly Justin laughed aloud. "On

second thought; not Roberta, I guess. Any woman who can stay calm while confronting crocodiles, who can not only take dictation at one hundred fifty words per minute but shinny up a palm tree like a native — well, she's obviously some different species who quite probably would never get sick; but it could have been I quite as easily as you, so don't give it another thought."

Flushing with pleasure at his words, Roberta grinned at Justin, but all too quickly he looked away, his grin fading and his face settling into the familiar scowl. Roberta could more or less understand Justin's apparent unhappiness. Devoted to his fiancée, he was stuck off here in Jamaica, rarely able to see her, stuck with dull routine work that never seemed to end, and never seemed to bring forth any answers. No wonder Justin was not optimistic anymore!

Eight days after Justin's return from Nassau, by which time Bill seemed fully recovered, they packed up the little green car once more and took off for the north coast area of Falmouth, where the lovely white beaches were thickly studded with coconut palms. Justin had considered flying but felt that after arriving at their destination they could more easily move around if they had a car. They had been to the north-beach area before, but the lab reports from their samples there were puzzling and inconclusive, so Justin felt they should return to that area for further work.

"The fact is," he admitted to Roberta as they drove, "at this point, in spite of all our hard work, we're still going around in circles, and I can hardly make even an educated guess as to which circle we should go back around again. But some instinct tells me the north coast is the most fruitful place to concentrate on, or maybe — it's only that the ocean and beach are so lovely there. Do you suppose that's all it is?"

Laughing softly, Roberta said, "Who knows?" and Justin momentarily laughed with her, but then he continued driving in silence.

They reached a stretch of beach that Justin seemed satisfied with late that afternoon, and after a dinner of fruits and fish, Bill reported that he felt a little tired, so he crawled into his sleeping bag and fell at once to sleep, while Justin dragged out his endless reports to study and Roberta went for a walk alone along the beach. The sun was just setting as she returned to where Justin was, and she noticed that he wasn't reading. He held his glasses in his hand and sat staring off at the waves.

Walking to a few feet from him, Roberta sat down cross-legged on the sand. She wore her usual daily attire, khaki shorts and T-shirt, her long hair tied back. Sitting down she reached up to untie her hair, letting it fall loose around her, then glanced at Justin and found him staring rather fixedly at her.

"Remember that night about three weeks ago," Justin said suddenly, "before we reached the Black River, when we spent a couple of nights along the southern coast and got to know that family, the couple with the two small children?"

"Wesley and Elizabeth? Of course I remember," Roberta answered, flooded with sudden memories of what a wonderful time they had had. Wesley and Elizabeth and their children had lived in a small but neat three-room wooden house, about a quarter of a mile inland from the southern beach. Wesley had come across them while they were working near the beach and had stopped to chat with them. Then, with a broad grin, he invited them to his home for dinner, an invitation they had gratefully accepted. After dinner they had all settled down on the small wooden porch of the house while Wesley and his wife, accompanied by two teen-age neighbor boys, had sung Calypso songs for them, accompanying themselves on a bamboo flute like instrument, and with hand-clapping on an old metal barrel. While their parents and friends were entertaining their guests, the two small children had crept closer and closer; then the little girl, an adorable child of two, had allowed herself to be pulled onto Roberta's lap. In time her older brother about three, had climbed on too, and Roberta had held both children, talking to them, playing with them, while the singing continued.

"Of course I remember," Roberta said again softly, her memory becoming even clearer. "That was really about the nicest evening we've spent here so far. They were so gracious and friendly, and the two children — I really enjoyed it."

"Me too," Justin said. "Not only did I enjoy it while we were there, but I keep finding myself thinking about it over and over again. At times I can't seem to put it out of my head."

"Like tonight?" Roberta suggested

softly, gazing thoughtfully at him. Justin was staring off now, toward the ocean. She heard him sigh.

"Yes, like tonight. You know, up to this point in my life I've never really given much thought to whether or not I wanted children. It wasn't that I felt I didn't want them. It's just something, as I say, that I'd never given any thought to. Then that night — well, after seeing you with those children, and such adorable children they were, and the way they crept onto your lap and you held them, talking with them — well, suddenly that night it hit me, after we'd left there and driven back and were settling down to sleep, well, suddenly it hit me that that's what I wanted. A family. I wanted children myself.

"Well, hell, I don't suppose there's anything odd in that. When a man reaches my age, has fallen in love and plans to get married, well, the closer the wedding day comes, naturally the more his thoughts are going to be drawn by what his life will be like after marriage. And that night I knew, more than ever, that what I want is to settle down and have a family."

Justin's eyes, which had been absently fixed on her, moved away as he sighed again. "So when I was in Nassau seeing Alicia, I mentioned it to her, that I would like to have a family pretty promptly after we get married. And the fact is, she didn't seem very pleased. While she agreed that some day she would of course have a child if that's what I want, I find myself doubting her word, not quite believing her; and somehow it's made me think a lot about her, and about our whole relationship, about the kind of person Alicia is, and the kind of woman I want for a wife."

Pausing again, Justin stood up, and, as though propelled by his movement, Roberta stood up too. They faced each other, a few feet apart.

"When I first met her three years ago," Justin suddenly began again, "I really fell hard for her. I thought her the most ravishingly beautiful woman I'd ever seen in my life, almost as though she couldn't possibly really exist, as though any moment I'd wake up again and find out she was only a dream, someone stepping miraculously out of some dream . . . "

Justin's voice died away, his eyes fastening on Roberta's. Then suddenly he was stepping toward her, his arms went around her. He pulled her against him, and his mouth came down on hers, kissing her more passionately than any man she'd ever known.

Taken completely by surprise, Roberta could scarcely breathe. She was painfully aware of Justin's closeness, his body pressing against hers, but didn't dare give herself up to the kiss, or let herself enjoy it. Instead she stayed tense and frightened, half trying to shrink back, to escape, while wanting, aching, to throw herself even more closely against him, to throw her arms around him and never, never let go.

But before she had done anything, before she could gather herself enough together to act, Justin's arms dropped, and without a word he strode rapidly away.

Roberta, sudden hot tears stinging her eyes, dropped down to her knees and buried her face in her hands. Why, she thought frantically, why doesn't he ever give me the chance to show how I feel? . . . He always surprises me and then runs away. Why can't he see what he means to me? And what am I supposed to do?

8

ONCE again there was a change in Justin's attitude toward her, Roberta felt, and it was not so subtle this time. Now back at work by the Rio Grande, he kept his distance but was no longer friendly; rather, he acted cold, hostile, unfriendly toward her. She couldn't be imagining it.

Also, things were evidently becoming strained between him and Alicia. A week ago when they'd returned to their hotel rooms in Kingston, there'd been a message from Alicia asking Justin to fly over a second time to spend time with her in Nassau, but Justin had phoned to tell her he couldn't make it; important reports were due in from the Miami lab that he wanted to get right on. There'd been at least six letters there from Alicia waiting for Justin — Roberta had seen the thick stack of her pink, perfumed envelopes — and Justin had scowled, sighing, as he'd taken them from the desk clerk. Why had he looked so upset, so unhappy? Possibly Justin's anger with her now was based upon some fear that if she, Roberta, were ever to see Alicia again, she'd let on that Justin had kissed her, or that he'd talked to her about his personal future plans.

Oh, if only she knew what it was, Roberta thought unhappily, there'd be some chance of smoothing things over, of reverting to their former friendliness, but when she really didn't know, could only wonder, fret about it, guess . . .

So the hell with it, Roberta told herself angrily at least ten times a day. So let Justin be angry with her, scowl at her, glare fiercely at her out of his dark eyes under those thick black brows! Whatever she'd done to upset him hadn't been intentional. She had done her best to get along with him and live up to what he expected of her, and if in some way she had failed him, as apparently she had, it was too bad! It was his own stupid fault for being so demanding, for having such impossibly high, rigid standards, and yet — yet Bill had repeatedly, over and over, failed to live up to what Justin wanted of him and not once had Justin gotten rude or mean to Bill. He'd always been friendly and understanding, he was *still* friendly with Bill! Why did she bear the brunt of his moods?

Roberta stopped working long enough to straighten up, press her hands to her hurting back, and swing around to stare fretfully out across the broad shallow river.

Oh, well, I suppose I'm feeling just as rude and snappish as Justin is, Roberta conceded after a moment, and with a sigh bent down to get back to work.

Even their evenings now, once a source of so much enjoyment and fun, had changed character and weren't enjoyable anymore. Gone were the times when Bill kept her laughing with his stories, now when they talked together after work it was in tense whispers, and almost always pertained to the dismal day they'd just had, or the dismal day they looked forward to.

"I honestly don't think he knows anymore what he's doing," Bill had whispered to her one night, edging close to her as they sat along the riverbank, his whisper low and muffled to make sure that Justin, who was studying more reports, couldn't possibly overhear.

"Bill don't say that!" Roberta wailed. "It's bad enough having to break our backs like this, but if it isn't even making sense to him — "

"Shush!" Bill cautioned, peeking fearfully over his shoulder. "For God's sake, don't let him hear."

"Oh, how could he possibly overhear?" Roberta protested, but even so she lowered her voice. It was always a surprise to her how clearly sounds traveled in this still warm air, and the last thing she wanted was to have Justin overhear.

They sat for a few moments in silence, then Bill repeated the same dismal thought. "Maybe we are detectives, as Justin said to start with, but if so we're now simply going round and round in circles, chasing after our own tails. And it's really eating that poor guy up. Have you noticed the way he barely picks at food anymore, and I don't think he's sleeping well either. Last night I heard him prowling around down here by the river — it must have been three o'clock. Can't eat, can't sleep — and can't figure out what in hell we should do next, which is why he's got us here, repeating ourselves. If you ask me, we should just cancel the whole project here and now and admit we're licked."

"Oh, Bill, no!" Roberta cried out, her voice rising in spite of herself. Instinctively they both glanced back to see if Justin had heard, but if so he gave no sign of it.

"And why not?" Bill argued. "If we

no longer know what we're doing, as I swear we don't, if we're just marking time, doing a lot of stupid busy work, why keep on? Don't tell me you enjoy this work just for the marvelous fun of doing it?"

"Of course not!" Roberta snapped, swinging to glare at Bill, feeling immediately angry. "But these palms *are* diseased; there is simply no denying that, which means something must be causing it, and until we find out what it is we should stay. Quite apart from the company's interest in finding out, just think of what a financial blessing it would be to Jamaica to have this blight brought under control! When this work is so terribly, terribly important, how can we throw in the towel now?"

"Because," Bill hissed at her, his thin freckled face moving closer to hers, "we are no longer accomplishing one damn thing, can't you get that through your head? We are simply wasting time, wasting the company's money, breaking our backs for nothing!

That's why we should call it off and forget the whole thing!"

"Quitter!" Roberta snapped, and jumping up in fury she strode off down the riverbank. Justin had been right from the first. Bill lacked something; he was a weakling, a coward, a rotten little quitter! Breathing hard, Roberta came to a stop along the bank where the tropical growth became so thick she couldn't continue on; for a moment, still in a fury, she considered diving into the river, clothes and all, to cool off. Both physically and emotionally she *needed* cooling off.

Grabbing a twig from a nearby bush, she began chewing on it, trying to relieve some of her anger that way. Even the river, such a source of wonder and delight to her during their first stay here, no longer soothed her as it had before. Though she continued to take her morning, noon, and evening dips, plunging in now she always took her troubles, her bad moods, her deep feeling of turmoil and imbalance, into the water with her — and in time came trudging out from each swim no more trouble-free than when she'd dived in. Oh, damn! Roberta thought, and pulling the twig from her mouth she angrily tossed it down.

Bill walked up slowly to where she stood, his thin face caught in a trouble frown. "Hey, Roberta, I'm sorry," he muttered. "I didn't mean to sound like that, or to get you upset. Can you forgive me?"

Momentarily Roberta wanted to snap back, 'I not only can't, I don't even *want* to. Just leave me alone!' but a moment later, she forced herself to glance around with a reasonably friendly smile.

"Sure, Bill, and I'm sorry I snapped at you too. I guess none of us is in a very good mood these days, and unfortunately we're beginning to take it out on each other, which just makes everything even worse."

"Right," Bill said, with a sudden grin. "But who else is there to take it out on? We're all feeling so damn frustrated. You and I are catching it from him, you know." Bill added, motioning back toward Justin, "He won't come right out and admit it, but he knows we're going around in circles, accomplishing nothing, and it's bugging the hell out of him. Then we pick it up from him and feel bugged too. That's the long and the short of it."

"You think so?" Roberta inquired thoughtfully, looking into Bill's lightly lashed green eyes.

"I know so," Bill said flatly. "I've worked with him before, remember, and when things are going well, it's great. He gets so friendly and appreciative there's no greater guy in the whole world, but when things go badly, as they're going now . . . " With a shrug, Bill let the thought complete itself.

After crawling into her sleeping bag that night, Roberta felt weighted down with the fear that she wouldn't be able to sleep. She'd been sleeping very badly of late, ever since the night more than two weeks before when Justin had kissed her so passionately, holding her close, only to run away without explanation.

Roberta forced herself to close her eyes, and she must have fallen into at least a light sleep, for sometime later she was startled out of a dream by the sound of steps, a man's rapid stride walking by, possibly twenty or thirty feet away. Staring out, she could make out a man's figure and knew at once that it was Justin. In the light from the nearly full moon, she watched him walk down toward the water's edge, then stand there unmoving. How strong he looked standing there, and yet how sad! Again tonight he apparently couldn't sleep.

On impulse Roberta drew her legs out of her bag and sat upon it. If she walked down to say hello, to tell Justin she couldn't sleep either . . . No, no, she shouldn't intrude on his privacy.

Besides which, he would simply take her head off for something, as he did so often these days. Or — would he kiss her again instead?

Abruptly, her heart all but bursting, Roberta knew that that's what would happen if she walked down to where he stood. He looked so tense and lonely standing there. If she got up, walked carefully and silently down to join him, when he turned to see her, for a moment he would stare at her, and then — then she would step closer and his arms would go around her and he would kiss her, as he had that other night, as he now had on two nights. Except that this time he would not release her so quickly again; this time he would stand there with his arms around her, holding her close, and their closeness would comfort him, possibly ease some of the tension out of him. And for her — for her it would be one more precious memory, one more moment carved out of time that she would never ever forget. So shouldn't she go?

"Yes. Yes, she *should*!

She made a slight movement to get up, then suddenly shivered, felt a cold wave pass over her, and changed her mind. What was she thinking of? She should stay right where she was.

If she went down there now and, instead of snapping at her or acting angry, he instead pulled her close and kissed her, how could that improve anything? The fact is it would only make matters worse. Angry at himself for again giving in to momentary temptation, for seeking comfort in human contact, in human closeness, Justin would simply become even more unbearable, more surly and bad tempered. He would blame *her* for being there. And he would be *right* in blaming her, if she walked down there for no other reason than the hope that he would give in to weakness and kiss her again.

So I must stay right here, Roberta

265

ordered herself, and with a sigh she leaned farther forward, resting her chin on her crossed arms, feeling a chill run through her. She looked over at Justin again, and she knew that she wanted more than anything to go to him. Why do I have to hold myself back? she thought sadly. I *want* Justin to kiss me, no matter what the consequences, no matter what it means — or doesn't mean — to him. If I were someone like Alicia, she decided, I wouldn't even hesitate for a minute. If I love him, he should know.

Thinking this, Roberta suddenly stood up, moving on impulse before she even realized she planned to, and the next moment she began picking her way barefooted over the rough ground, watching her feet as she walked, a tiny smile playing around her mouth. However Justin reacted to her — well, he looked so lonely standing there, and she was lonely too, sleepless as he was, why shouldn't they reach out to one another for whatever comfort there might be? To be alone with him for just a few moments, however it worked out, was all she could ask for.

Suddenly, she heard a man's stride approaching her; her eyes shot up and there was Justin, walking toward her. As Roberta stopped walking, her heart pounding so hard it threatened to burst, Justin seemed suddenly to see her, to become aware of her there, and taken completely by surprise, he stopped walking too. They stood in the bright moonlight, both of them silent and unmoving.

In time Justin spoke, his voice clipped and crisp as usual, but not unfriendly. "Well, Roberta, you can't sleep either?"

"No, no, I couldn't," Roberta murmured, beginning to tremble slightly, furious at herself for doing so. "Mainly nerves, I guess, and the fact that I'm overly tired."

"Yes," Justin agreed, "the same with me, no doubt." There was silence for a moment, then Justin began walking toward her, almost reaching her side before he stopped. Again he stood staring at her, then his eyes circled away and he bit his lip.

"You know what I was just thinking of doing," Justin said next. "It's a lovely night with a nearly full moon, and apparently I'm too keyed to sleep, too worried about too many things. The river looks so calm and soothing, so what I was thinking of doing was getting on the raft and going for a ride on the river." Justin paused, his eyes circling back to meet hers. "Will you join me?" he asked in a soft, hushed voice. "Please?"

"Oh, no, I don't think so," Roberta answered quickly, her voice quivering, almost breaking. "If Bill were to wake and find us both gone . . . " A feeble excuse but the first one she could think of, standing there in the moonlight trembling so badly she half feared she might fall apart. But — why did she need an excuse, why didn't she just accept Justin's invitation and go with him for a moonlight ride on the river? What was she afraid of?

Oh, don't believe me, Justin, I do want to go after all! Roberta thought wildly an instant later, but she knew it was already too late. Immediate anger had flashed through Justin's eyes and his face closed up.

"As you wish," he said coldly. "Please excuse me for even suggesting it." With these words he strode on by, eyes down, leaving Roberta standing there, feeling faint with nausea and regret.

★ ★ ★

When she next saw Justin, the following morning, his eyes momentarily stared straight at her, filled with fury and scorn, and then for the rest of the day he scarcely glanced her way. When forced to speak to her, he did so as tersely as possible, his eyes avoiding hers, his manner openly hostile, his rudeness so apparent that even Bill noticed.

"Boy, the boss man's sure got it in for you today," he whispered to her about two that afternoon as they worked side by side labeling samples. "What did you do, accidentally let some sweat drop on one of his precious reports?"

"Something like that," Roberta murmured in answer, forcing a weak little smile. "But as you said yesterday, I think the main thing is how frustrated he's beginning to feel over our lack of progress. That's the thing that's really bothering him."

And because Justin felt this deep-down frustration, Roberta reasoned with herself, he had issued that invitation to her last night, wanting to use her, the only woman who was handy, to ease his frustration a little by — by what? Making love to her on the raft? Is that what he'd had in mind? Probably not, or at least not consciously, but quite possibly that's what he'd hoped for unconsciously, or rather, that's what his frustrations might have sought. So today he was angry at her for not relieving those pent-up frustrations, whereas if she'd accepted his invitation and had offered him the comfort and solace he so sought, today he would be furious with her for *that*.

Which means there was no way I could win, Roberta concluded, smiling even more grimly to herself. From the moment that Justin had first really looked at her — had it happened in the corridor of the hotel in Ocho Rios at Christmas, had that been the first time he had? — from that moment on, the kind of angry, no-win situation they were in now had no doubt been inevitable. No wonder he had given her his word back in Los Angeles that he would never once think of her as a woman!

So the real problem is that I fell in love with Justin, Roberta admitted, one long last sigh running through her. No doubt she'd done the right thing, the only possible thing, in refusing his invitation of the night before, so she might as well forget it. In the bright light of day, reason prevailed.

Two days later, Justin announced tersely at breakfast that they were packing up and leaving as there was little more that could be accomplished there. As he spoke, his voice grew thick and almost cracked. Glancing quickly at him, Roberta noticed with shock how thin he looked, his face drawn and lined, his clothes hanging rather loosely on him. His dark eyes now looked cloudy and dull.

Oh, I can't stand it, Roberta thought, *seeing him like this!* She could no longer doubt Bill's contention that their failure in pinning down the cause of the blight was the primary reason for the change in Justin. He might in addition be worried about his engagement to Alicia, might be angry at her, Roberta, for various things, but the thing that was upsetting him the most was their investigative failure.

"Is there nothing more we can do then?" Roberta asked softly, with deep compassion, not caring that she was giving Justin one more chance to answer with scorn or take her head off.

But this time, he didn't. Instead his eyes momentarily met hers as he said coolly, "Oh, we'll find other things to try, don't worry. There's no way we'll quit trying until the very last minute, until time runs completely out." He lifted his head a little higher as he turned to walk away.

Daunted but not yet defeated, Roberta thought, watching him stride rapidly off. Until time ran out, until there wasn't another moment left — even if all they were doing now was running around in circles, chasing after their own tails, as Bill had said.

The days that followed fled by in a whirlwind of never-ending activity, but how much of it served any purpose at all, Roberta couldn't tell. Bill claimed it was now desperation time; they were moving so swiftly, so perpetually, to keep from having to face that they were in actuality standing completely still, accomplishing absolutely nothing.

If only there were some way I could help! Roberta found herself thinking night after sleepless night, but she knew there was no way she could. If she reached out to Justin to offer comfort, he would only hate her afterwards, and hate himself even more. There was no way to go along now other than as they were, barely on speaking terms, with every day that dawned a little more like total strangers, like two people who had never shared a friendly moment. Justin, seemingly now totally absorbed in his own frustrations, no longer snapped at her as he had, or glared angrily at her; rather, he now acted as though she didn't even exist, as though nothing existed for him any more apart from his painful awareness of total, crushing defeat.

Four days before the assignment was due to wind up, before Justin would have to call it off if he was going to make it to New York City for his wedding, they were working on the southern coast, about half a day's drive from Kingston. At Justin's insistence they had left their hotel just before daybreak, had driven at a furious pace along the coast, and then Justin had suddenly swerved the car off the road and announced that they were going to check out a few palms in the area. The beach was a narrow, rock-strewn one, the day was already muggy and warm, and as they worked steadily through the long boring hours, Roberta found herself becoming as inwardly rebellious as Bill seemed to be. If what they were doing had any point — but she had begun to lose all faith that it did. And to slave away like this, if it was totally pointless . . .

About four that afternoon it began to rain, rather haphazardly at first, in large, scattered drops. Bill, walking over to kneel beside Roberta, remarked, "Maybe if it starts raining hard enough, the boss will let us knock off and go home," grinning rather good-naturedly as he said it.

"You know better than that," Roberta answered, smiling too. "How does it go — 'Neither rain nor sleet nor hail nor dark of night — '"

"Yeah, but we're not carrying the U.S. mail," Bill argued, laughing, his hand for one moment coming down to rest affectionately on Roberta's arm. "All we're doing is gunning our motors for no reason at all."

"Bill, would you kindly stop saying that!" Roberta responded rather sharply, suddenly irritated by his insistence on this. "You don't know that and neither do I. If Justin thinks what we're doing is necessary and important — "

At the mention of his name, they both instinctively glanced around, looking for him. Not seeing him, Roberta raised her eyes and located him climbing a palm some sixty or seventy feet away, already nearing the top. She narrowed her eyes, thinking to herself that the tree looked like a healthy one — but who could tell? Just as Justin had said, maybe every single tree on the island was already diseased, with some simply not showing any symptoms yet, which meant that in trying to track down a parasite present in some of the trees but not in others, or in trying to pin down some subtle difference in environment between apparently healthy trees and obviously blighted ones . . . Oh, how could they hope to win out against a disease so elusive, with so many variable factors involved? It seemed hopeless.

As the afternoon wore on the rain grew heavier, and then, without warning, a brisk wind blew up. Roberta first became aware of it as she straightened up once and found to her surprise that the wind almost blew her over. Stiffening against it, she glanced around for Bill and Justin, but saw neither one nearby. She took one step from where she'd been working crouched down, and as she did so the wind all but toppled her over. Suddenly frightened, she looked up and stared in openmouthed fascination at what she saw: thick black clouds darkening the sky over the ocean, sweeping inland.

The next moment, before she'd had time to take it all in, an even mightier wind blew in and sent her crashing down to the ground. Concerned about the earth and water samples she had spent the whole day collecting, Roberta tried to lift herself up onto her knees, only to be smashed immediately down to the ground again. Then feeling utterly helpless, she was lifted by a great gust and carried several feet, then thrown down against the base of a palm tree.

For the first time real fear struck her. What kind of a wind was this that it could toss her around like this, as though she were little more than a piece of bamboo? Breathing hard, already soaked through with the slashing, furious rain, Roberta threw her arms around the base of the palm tree to brace herself, trying to consider what was the best thing for her to do. If she could possibly make it to the car, she might be all right.

Thinking this, she glanced around in the direction of the car, located it, saw it actually being lifted, swooped up with as much ease as she herself had been. Then it was dumped down again on the beach, where it tumbled over onto one side, then turned upside down. If the wind could do that to the car, what was in store for them?

Thoroughly frightened now, Roberta tried to press herself more heavily to the ground and to hold on to the palm tree even harder, but this didn't suffice. A moment later the wind again reached under her and lifted her up, first her feet and legs, then her torso, last of all her head and arms, and again she went whirling away in the air, tossed about like a tiny stick, only to be thrown down again several yards away on the beach.

Panting in terror, Roberta tried to clutch onto the shifting sand, to somehow press her body into the sand, though she knew that was pointless. What hope was there, what was the best thing to do? To stay where she was, in the open, to be constantly swept up and thrown about . . . ?

Staring around her, she saw that about fifteen feet from where she lay was an immature palm, its base small enough, possibly, for her to get her arms completely around. If she could crawl over there, wrap herself around the tree, cling for dear life — she might have a chance.

Lifting her head, she looked up at the fierce dark sky pouring down its heavy, punishing rain, the wind over her head roaring by with thunderous noise, with the force, it seemed, of a hurricane.

That was it, Roberta suddenly realized, *they'd been caught in a hurricane!* If she could just crawl over to that palm . . .

Too frightened to try to get up, even onto her knees, Roberta began pushing herself forward across the rough, rocky sand with swimming motions. Once, as she felt the wind sweep down and threaten to pick her up again, she stopped moving and pressed down as hard as she could. For once, in mercy, the wind swept on by without whirling her up. Finally, finally, she made it across the sand and reached out to grab the palm.

At first she lay straight out, her arms around the base of the palm, but, remembering how the wind had pulled her effortlessly away from that other tree, she pushed herself in closer, wrapping herself more securely around the base, circling her body around it, holding on for dear life.

Still breathing hard, still terribly frightened and confused, Roberta lay curled up around the base of the palm, for the most part keeping her eyes closed, trying not to think. Slowly she became aware that her body hurt, that she was bleeding in various spots — her legs, her arms, her buttocks — but it seemed to her that, in spite of the buffeting flights she had taken, ending with hard smashes back to earth, she hadn't broken any bones or suffered any permanent damage — she hoped!

Then something almost as startling, almost as frightening as her first toss into the air happened: a hand suddenly grabbed onto her arm, fiercely clutching it.

Startled nearly out of her wits, Roberta opened her eyes, and even in the menacing darkness could see who it was: Justin, reaching out to clasp her arm, Justin with his thick black hair tumbled down on his brow, his face bleeding along both cheeks, Justin looking at her with haunted dark eyes, then crawling the rest of the way to her, circling his body around behind hers, his arms going over hers to grab onto the palm, his bleeding face pressing in against her shoulder.

"Oh, God, Roberta," Justin panted into her ear, his voice thick and choked, "I saw you lifted up once, straight into the air, then I couldn't see you anywhere. I was nearly out of my mind. Are you all right?"

"Fine, fine," Roberta responded, in the next moment almost laughing, for how fine was she? Scared half to death, bruised and bleeding, soaked through and afraid to move, yet now, now with Justin's strong body pressed in close against hers, his arms around her, she felt almost calm, certainly much less afraid.

"You picked yourself a great spot," Justin yelled into her ear over the thunder of the storm. "We should be able to ride it out right here."

"How about Bill?" Roberta yelled back.

"He's okay," Justin shrieked back, "down in a hole." Then, as a fresh, fierce wind suddenly crept in under them and lifted them inches off the ground, they turned their attention to holding on to the palm with all their strength.

"We'll make it through all right," he said, and Roberta knew he was right. Pressed together like this, his strength added to hers, they would make it through just fine.

As the wind swept down again and again, maniacal in its fury, and the low, black sky poured a torrent of rain upon them, Roberta felt little of the lash of the storm, for her heart had never felt such joy, such bursting happiness. She'd seen Justin's eyes — the look in his eyes — when he'd found her here, alive and uninjured, and could no longer doubt that he cared for her, could no longer doubt the depth and power of that caring. His eyes had seemed to say, in fact, that had circumstances been different, had there been no Alicia, *he might even have fallen in love with her!*

9

JUSTIN was leaving the following day by commercial flight to go to New York for his wedding. He had already returned the light private plane to the Jamaican government. The hurricane had rendered their little green car undrivable; the Jamaican official with whom Justin was dealing graciously offered to put another car at their disposal, but Justin had courteously declined, saying it wasn't needed.

When the hurricane had at last drenched and buffeted them with its final fury and had whirled on out to sea again they had managed to make it home by flagging down a friendly Jamaican passing by in a van, a man who'd been happy to taxi them to their hotel in Kingston for a modest fee. After an exhausted night's sleep, they'd rented a car in the morning and had gone back to the scene of the wreckage to salvage what they could of their equipment, finding very little that was unharmed. With much heaving and the use of sturdy bamboo poles as levers, they'd managed to right the car, only to find that it wouldn't start. So they'd unloaded it and, with reluctance abandoned it there.

"Well, this effectively puts an end to any further investigative effort," Justin had muttered. "Which doesn't matter. Time had run out on us anyway. The only thing left to do is file our reports and forget the whole thing."

In this somber and defeated mood they had driven back, in almost total silence, to the Sheraton-Kingston.

Of the three of them, only Bill seemed not to feel depressed and gloomy. Though he said very little and seemed to be trying to keep any smiles or grins off his face, Roberta sensed that he was feeling anything but down; that, in fact, he felt exceptionally excited and elated, which she found herself resenting. If Bill felt so happy simply because of Justin's defeat — well, he wasn't much of a friend, or even a decent human being, if he could take such joy in this depressing end to all their arduous labors.

But after they'd returned to the hotel and Justin left to go see the Jamaican official about the car, Roberta found she had been accusing Bill unjustly in her thoughts. He wasn't feeling elated because of the ill-fated end of their endeavors, but rather because of some mail that he'd found waiting for him at the hotel upon their return the previous evening, following their successful endurance of the hurricane.

She'd barely reached her room when Bill rang her up on the phone, asking if he could come see her about something, a formality which would have amused Roberta a little if she hadn't felt too depressed to find anything amusing.

"Of course, come on over if you like. I'm not doing a thing but sitting here staring at the floor, feeling lousy."

Bill laughed. "Maybe what I want to discuss with you will cheer you up a bit. I hope so, anyway. Be right there."

Seconds later Roberta heard the knock on her door and called out, "Come in." As Bill walked in, she was flooded with the memory of the first time he had dropped by her room, the day they had met, her first day here in Jamaica, and Bill's dire words of warning about what an impossible man Justin was to work for. And now the assignment was over, Justin due to leave for New York and his scheduled wedding to Alicia. Roberta felt tears flood into her eyes but she hastily blinked them back, doing her best to smile at Bill as he walked in grinning at her.

To her surprise Bill walked directly to her, to where she sat disconsolately on the end of the bed, grabbed hold of her by the arms and pulled her to her feet, planting a firm kiss on her mouth. Then his arms went around her and he held her to him, still not saying anything.

Roberta, in spite of her best efforts at control felt fresh hot tears well up and threaten to spill over. Bill's arms felt warm, comforting — but the day before, during the hurricane, it had been Justin's arms around her, Justin holding her close, pressed against her from head to toe. Twice during that fearfully black hour, while the wind howled furiously over their heads and the rains lashed murderously down on them, Justin had even kissed her, pressing a kiss once on the side of her throat, the other kiss against her cheek.

After his first kiss on her throat, she had struggled to turn her head around to face him, wanting, aching, to feel his mouth pressing one last time on hers, but they were wedged in so tightly together, smashed so hard against the soaked earth, she couldn't turn her head far enough and Justin, with what sounded like a little sigh had pressed the second kiss on her cheek. They'd seemed to have no choice but to settle for that. But then, when the winds finally died down, when the rain let up a bit, when the fierce darkness overhead seemed to lighten somewhat as the worst of the storm moved on . . .

Well, when that happened, when Justin had at last judged it was all right to move again, at first they had pulled up into a sitting position, facing each other, Justin's hands holding hers; and his eyes had met hers directly, his dark eyes looking straight across into hers as he'd held her hands, holding them very hard, and then he'd said, 'You'll never know, sweetheart, how relieved I was when I found you here. I was terrified that you'd been blown out to sea,' and then the next moment he had leaned forward and kissed her on the mouth, not hard and passionately as he'd kissed her before, but gently, warmly, tenderly, a kiss that had sent shivers of delight running through her.

Drawing back, Justin had again looked steadily across at her, then had murmured, 'Well, I guess we'd better go check on Bill,' and the next moment he had jumped to his feet, had reached down to help her up, and the magic moment — the moment in which he had called her 'sweetheart' and had kissed her with such feeling — was over; they were simply co-workers again, two comrades whose job it was to go immediately in search of the third member of their party.

With tears overflowing her eyes and beginning to run down her cheeks, Roberta remembered all this — as Bill, holding her close, suddenly chuckled to himself.

Drawing back, Roberta gently released herself from Bill's hold, trying to turn away quickly enough, so that Bill wouldn't see her tears. As she walked quickly over to her dresser to grab up a tissue to dry her eyes and blow her nose, Roberta said, "Well, Mr. Coffer, you certainly seem in a festive mood. Are you this happy simply because our assignment is now all but over?" While my heart is breaking for that very reason, Roberta added to herself, but didn't say. She swung back from the dresser to face Bill directly, trying not to feel resentful and scornful that he was reacting this way. Surely he was not at all her kind of people, just as Justin had said.

But Bill's face immediately lost his happy grin at her words and he protested at once, "No, no, Roberta, for Pete's sake that's not it. What kind of a guy do you take me for anyway? I'm not saying that my heart's completely broken to have it drawing to a close, but I'm not feeling happy about it either. If we'd been successful that would be different; I'd feel great about everything, but the way things are — well, hell, I feel as rotten as you do that in the end all of our work came to nothing, and if there were any way in the world I could change that . . . But there isn't, so why should I brood about it, anymore than I can help anyway? But the thing that's making me feel so good . . . "

"Yes?" Roberta prodded when Bill, grinning, running his hand over his bright red hair, hesitated a moment.

"Well, the fact is," Bill exploded a moment later, "I got this letter from a college in California — from Orange County, California, just south of where you live. Well, this letter was here waiting for me when we got back yesterday, and it's an answer to an application I put in there — I've been hired there as a teacher beginning with the next quarter, which starts in June! Isn't that great? Oh, Roberta, can't you see how fantastic this is!"

Again Bill was upon her, grinning, his arms going around her to draw her close. Again he kissed her, then whispered into her ear, "A permanent teaching job means I'll be able to give up this kind of short assignment, which I loathe anyway. From now on I can settle down and start building my life."

Bill kissed her again, then drew back, again grinning at her. Slowly his grin faded away a bit as he said, "Roberta, sweetheart, have you given any more thought to what we discussed that night in Ocho Rios? Surely by now you have given more thought to it and can see how sensible, how *right* it would be! Look at how well we get along, how compatible we are, and there's no one in the whole world that I respect and admire as I respect and admire you. Oh, darling, won't you please agree to marry me?"

As Bill stepped forward again, reaching out with his long thin arms to draw her close, Roberta couldn't stop herself from beginning to cry all over again, in little gulping sobs this time as Bill held her close, pressing an occasional comforting kiss on her brow or cheek — so meaningless compared to Justin's kisses of the day before! Yet that shouldn't be so, she shouldn't *allow* it to be so!

Struggling to control her tears, Roberta again drew free, saying in a voice that faltered and broke, "but, Bill, I — I just don't think I love you that much, enough to marry you. I am fond of you, terribly fond . . . " She walked quickly to her dresser to grab up a tissue, hopefully to dry her eyes.

"I know that," Bill said, sounding not the least perturbed. "I know just what the problem is. Don't think I don't. Right now you're in love with Justin, or think you are. No use trying to deny it, Roberta, because I'm not as dumb and blind as all that. Right now you're so infatuated with him that's all you can think about. You think he's the only man in the world, the only man worth loving, the only man you'd ever want to marry — "

"But — but, Bill, if you know that, if you understand how I feel, then I don't understand — "

"That's right, you don't understand!"

Bill cried out, again hurrying to her, to try to draw her close, but this time Roberta resisted and wouldn't be drawn into the circle of his arms.

Giving in, not wanting to force her, Bill stood a moment holding her by the arms, his eyes probing hers. "What you don't understand, what you're blind to right now, because of this infatuation you feel for him, is that we could still have a very satisfactory marriage, a very happy one in spite of your claim that you don't love me. Now I know perfectly well that you're not as wildly in love with me as you are with him, but even if Justin loved you too, what kind of marriage could you have with him? You know I think very highly of him — there's no man on earth I more greatly respect and admire — but if you look at him calmly and realistically you have to face the fact that he is a very intense and high-strung man, like a candle burning at both ends — he's bound to burn himself out before too long."

Bill paused a moment, then, moving his head to toss back his hair he added, his eyes holding Roberta's, "But I'm not like that. I pace myself, so my love for you will last us both a lifetime if only you'll let it."

After saying this, Bill leaned forward and pressed a soft kiss on Roberta's mouth, then drew away, grinning.

"Another thing, Roberta. You'd like to have children, wouldn't you? Most women would. Well, think about that. Justin's whole life is traveling, three months here, four months there, six months at the other side of the earth. If somehow you were to marry him, somehow get him to drop Alicia and marry you instead, once you have children you wouldn't be able to travel with him anymore, and wouldn't that leave you lonely? Surely a husband who has a nice steady permanent job in one place, a husband who'll be there all the time, home every night for dinner and every weekend, week in and week out, is better than a husband who spends his life leaving you, jumping here and there all over the place, isn't he?"

"Well . . . " Roberta murmured, aware that her tears were at last drying up. What Bill said made a lot of sense, and besides . . . Well, in any case this entire conversation was completely unrealistic anyway, as it wasn't as though she had to make a choice between the two men. In one more day, in less than thirty hours, Justin would be flying off to marry the woman he loved. Alicia was the one who'd have to struggle with the problems of an intense, high-strung husband who constantly left her to go flying off on job assignments. Alicia, not her.

"This is an idiotic conversation!" Roberta said, trying to snap the words out sharply, but her voice betrayed her and she found herself close to tears again; still she struggled to add, "It's not as though I'm making any choice between the two of you. Justin hasn't the least interest in me, and we both know perfectly well he's marrying Alicia!"

"Right!" Bill exclaimed. "I'm delighted to hear you say that. I didn't want to be the one to point it out, but, Roberta, it's true; and since you can't have Justin, the man you think right now you love, why won't you give serious consideration to marrying me? We could build a good, solid marriage, I know we could, and you'd learn to love me in time. So please, darling, marry me!"

As Bill drew her close again, kissing her, Roberta felt something in herself give a little, and she told herself that maybe she should pay attention to what Bill was saying. Since she couldn't have the man she wanted, shouldn't she settle — and settle happily — for a man she was truly fond of, with whom she felt very comfortable, a man who had already proved he could amuse and entertain her?

Thinking this, Roberta tried to let go of her tensions, to relax in Bill's embrace and give herself up to enjoying his kiss. Doing this, she didn't at first hear the sudden, sharp rap on her door; then a moment later the door opened and someone stepped in.

Startled, Roberta immediately opened her eyes, which she'd closed in an attempt to enjoy Bill's kiss, and over Bill's shoulder she found herself staring at a surprised, embarrassed-looking Justin.

"Sorry," Justin murmured, turning away, his cheeks flushing pink. "Terribly sorry. I thought I heard you say come in."

Bill, letting go of Roberta and quickly swinging around, responded at once, "No need to apologize, Justin, nor to feel embarrassed. What you've just witnessed was our engagement kiss. Roberta and I are getting married."

Smiling triumphantly, Bill walked over to Justin, sticking out his hand. "So congratulate me, old man. I know you wish us every happiness."

"Of course, naturally." Justin rather

awkwardly took Bill's hand to shake. His eyes reached over to face Roberta. "And my best wishes to you, Roberta. I hope you'll be very happy."

"Thank you," Roberta murmured, feeling her own face flush.

"Well, I've got things to do," Bill exclaimed happily. "Want to send a wire off to California at once to accept a job I was just offered, and I know you two have things to do too, winding up the reports, etc., so I'll see you both later." Blowing Roberta a happy kiss, Bill strode to the door and let himself out.

There was an awkward silence for several seconds, Roberta not knowing what to say, her face growing warmer and warmer as Justin stood looking silently across at her.

"Well — did you want to get right down to work?" Roberta asked falteringly at length. "I know we still have a stack of reports to complete and send in."

Justin made a little movement as

though dismissing this, then said rather sharply in his clear, crisp voice, "So you've decided to marry him after all. That was something I didn't expect."

Her cheeks on fire, Roberta turned half away, answering with a nervous little laugh, "No, no, I haven't decided yet, one way or another. We were just discussing it, that's all, when you walked in."

"Discussing it in a rather physical way, from what I observed!" Justin commented tartly, his voice edged with scorn. "And Bill seems to have no doubts that he's won you over. What was that job offer he was talking about?"

Roberta nervously pulled at the damp tissue she held in her hands, feeling her inner tension increase. "Oh, it's a permanent teaching position he applied for some time after we arrived here. There was a letter waiting for him yesterday that he can have the job, so he feels very happy and pleased about that. He'd rather settle down in one place than lead the kind of life you do, traveling about on various job assignments."

"Yes, I know." After a slight pause Justin added, his voice even colder and more filled with scorn, "So now you two can settle down together right there in your home state and enjoy all the blessings of wedded bliss. In view of all the facts, I repeat my sincere congratulations to you both. And now — if you can bring your mind back to more mundane things — possibly we can get on with our work?"

"Of course," Roberta agreed. "Here or in your room?"

At last she found the courage to face Justin directly, to meet, unflinchingly, his dark eyes staring across at her. Well, she couldn't live her whole life to please one impossible man! she told herself in immediate answering fury. In all truth, whether she married Bill or didn't marry him was no particular business of Justin's! In one more day his work here would be done; he'd be flying off to marry the woman he loved, leaving her behind to pick up the pieces of her life — and if she wished to share her life with Bill, a man she was truly fond of, that decision was up to her, and let Justin think what he pleased about it!

"My room, please," Justin responded in an even colder, more hostile voice. "I'll expect you in five minutes." With that he turned on his heel and walked rapidly to the odor.

With a sigh Roberta watched him go, telling herself she didn't feel fresh hurting tears sting her eyes. Well, all right, so what if she did? No one had ever claimed it was easy to part from a man you were in love with, even when the man didn't return your love. Maybe it hurt even more when you knew perfectly well the man didn't love you.

In less than five minutes Roberta was tapping lightly on Justin's door and soon heard his voice call out for her to come in. For the rest of the day, and for hours the following morning, Justin dictated endless reports to her, detailing the disappointing results of their three months' investigation.

Throughout their long hours of work, not for a single minute did a very formal coldness give way between them. Not once did Justin make any kind of personal comment, and Roberta followed suit, speaking only when absolutely necessary in a cool tone, while her heart ached miserably. He had no right to be angry with her, Roberta thought repeatedly, no matter what she decided to do with regard to marrying Bill. That was her business, her life, and who was Justin to think he could dictate to her about it? In this way she matched his anger with an answering anger of her own, and hour after hour they worked together without ever exchanging a pleasant or friendly glance or word.

At two in the afternoon, after Justin completed his dictation and they ate a light lunch, Roberta and

Bill accompanied him by taxi to the airport to see him off. Only Bill seemed unaffected by the angry chill in the air. They were so late getting to the airport that there was little time for pleasantries, and by the time Justin had checked his luggage and gotten his seat assignment, it was time to board the plane — which is probably the way he'd planned it, Roberta thought sadly; this way they could come closer to avoiding last-minute awkwardness.

"Well, this is it," Justin commented just before turning to leave. He stuck out his hand to Bill. "Thanks, Bill, for everything, and I hope your new job is to your liking and that you and Roberta are wonderfully happy."

His freckled face flushing, Bill grinned, shaking hands, murmuring, "Well, thank you, sir, and the same to you."

For a moment Roberta felt sure — and her heart dove down sickly with the thought — that Justin was going to turn away and go down the ramp onto the plane without so much as saying good-bye to her, without even glancing her way. She saw him half turn away to do just that, but then at the last moment he turned back to face her. Tears stinging her eyes, Roberta put out her hand.

"Good-bye, Justin" — her voice breaking in spite of herself. "Thank you for everything and I — I hope you and Alicia will be very, very happy."

Justin didn't answer for a moment. He stood looking at her, staring at her; then, though his hand caught hers and held it, at the same time he put his other arm around her and rather awkwardly drew her close, pressing a kiss on her brow.

"Good-bye, beautiful one," he murmured, then pressed another quick kiss on her brow. The next second he had swung around and was striding hurriedly down the ramp to board the plane.

Watching him go, Roberta began to cry, wanting desperately to draw him back, to dissolve the hostility of the last two days in a truly warm good-bye — but Justin *had* been wrong in trying to dictate her life!

After she and Bill caught a taxi back to the hotel, Roberta found she felt too tired, too dispirited to begin typing up the endless shorthand notes she had taken. Though she and Bill had already booked flights to Miami for the following afternoon, she told him at dinner that she couldn't possibly finish up her work and leave that soon. The way she was feeling it might take her two or three days to finish the reports. She couldn't see any sense in pushing herself.

"Alright," Bill answered gaily, reaching across to touch her hand. "I agree with you; now that the slave driver's gone, why knock yourself out? The only thing that would accomplish is driving you into an early grave. So we'll cancel our reservations, you take all the time you like, and whenever you've finished we'll fly back together, no problem at all."

Roberta took a deep breath, lifted her

eyes, and faced the redhead directly, her eyes insistently catching his.

"No, Bill, that's not the way I'd like it to be," her voice soft but firm. "I've thought everything over very carefully, everything you asked me to consider when you proposed again, and I'm sure that everything you said makes very good sense; but I'm just not ready to marry you, and because I'm not, and because of the way I feel right now, so emotionally exhausted, I don't want to see a single familiar face. You'd be doing me a tremendous favor if you'd go ahead and fly out tomorrow as planned. Would you do that for me, Bill, please?"

Bill's freckled face had grown pale as she talked, but his eyes didn't move from hers. After a moment he said, "It hurt that much to lose him then, even though you knew all along that you were going to, that you had to say good-bye to him?"

Tears flooding into her eyes, Roberta nodded. "Yes, it hurts that much, even more than I thought it would, and now all I want is to crawl into a corner somewhere, all by myself. Can you understand that, Bill?"

"Yes," Bill said, "I can understand. And if that's what you want, that's what I'll do. I wouldn't want to cause you any more pain."

The following afternoon, not too long after lunch, Roberta caught a cab with Bill to accompany him to the airport to see him off. As Bill kissed her good-bye, Roberta momentarily wondered, with a slight touch of panic, whether she was doing the right thing, whether she'd reached the right decision. But the next moment the panic died away and she knew she had. She couldn't marry a man she didn't really love, as fond as she was of Bill. If she never fell in love again, then possibly she would simply never marry. In any case, until the memory of Justin stopped haunting her, stopped hurting her, she couldn't even think of loving someone else.

But Bill was a very nice guy and

she truly appreciated how well he had taken her final refusal to marry him. As he kissed her one last time, she kissed him warmly. Then he was walking away up the ramp, as Justin had the day before, and she was alone. Of the three of them who had started here three months before, she alone was left. Left with the task of winding up all the loose ends.

Returning to her hotel, she found she still didn't feel like getting down to work, so she read for a while and napped. In the morning, possibly in the morning, she would deal with her work.

After breakfast the following day, Roberta finally felt able to tackle the work that was left to do. In his final report, summarizing their investigation, Justin had wound up by saying that the only possible course of action he could recommend to the Jamaican government was that they uproot every coconut palm on the entire island whether yet struck by the blight or not, wait a minimum of five years, then replant healthy seed. Which of course, he had added in his report to the home office, he knew that Jamaica couldn't possibly afford to do and wouldn't do.

As she set up her typewriter and prepared to type out this report and several others, Roberta sighed over the uselessness of all they had done. She flipped through some of the endless lab reports they had gotten back from Miami, reporting on the endless specimens they had sent in for analysis. Surely somewhere in this stack of reports there had to be a worthwhile clue, something to go on, some lead. But apparently there hadn't been or at least Justin hadn't been able to find one.

Sighing, Roberta set up her steno pad, rolled paper into her machine, and began to type. If she stayed at it steadily she might be able to finish by evening, and then she could book a flight out for the following day.

Plunging into work, Roberta stopped thinking, became a living machine whose eyes and hands became co-ordinated without need for conscious control as her eyes moved over her notes and her fingers flew across the typewriter keyboard. Then suddenly, startling her so that she jerked, there was a sharp rap on her bedroom door, and the next moment the door flew open and a man came striding in.

Justin!

But — Roberta saw as she stared open mouthed — not the defeated, gray-faced, tired-looking Justin who had left here two days before; but rather the bright-eyed, glowing, superbly fit looking Justin of three months ago, the man she had first met and fallen in love with. Justin walked rapidly across the room, grinning, reaching her machine and pulling the paper out, tearing it up as she sat staring in utter befuddlement.

"Forget this," Justin ordered, in his clear, crisp voice. He grabbed her steno pad and began ripping out the pages of that too, sending the torn pieces fluttering down to the floor. "Forget all this garbage. This job isn't over yet, and won't be over until we've pinned down the cause of the blasted blight and found some way to cure the palms."

Tossing the steno pad down too, he stepped around the table on which the typewriter was sitting, and grabbing Roberta by both arms pulled her up and soundly kissed her, his mouth pressing hard on hers.

When he released her at last, when she could breathe again, Roberta stuttered, "But — but what happened, Justin? Alicia agreed you could come back?"

"Alicia and I came to an agreement, all right," Justin responded, grinning. "That we aren't right for each other, never will be right for each other, and have no business even thinking of getting married. I used to look at her and think she was the most beautiful woman alive. Now I look at her and I don't see that at all. I see all the hours she has spent grooming her hair, pampering her face, putting on her makeup just so. Three months ago I still thought of her as exquisitely beautiful, but as I was flying away from here the other day, you know what happened? All I could think of was you, your lovely suntanned face, thick shining wet hair streaming down your back, the way you walk, head high, proud . . . "

"Oh, hell, let's just say I fell out of love with Alicia and deeply into love with someone else, a woman I can share my work with as well as my life, and let it go at that."

"But — but — " Roberta stuttered, her head still whirling with confusion, her eyes searching the bright gleaming ones gazing so happily into hers.

"But? But what?" Justin responded, laughing. "Once I'd had it out with Alicia, I phoned the hotel here last night, asked for Bill, was told he had already checked out while you were still here so here I am. Will you marry me, sweetheart?"

Not waiting for an answer, Justin kissed her again, his lips pressing passionately on hers, with a new certainty, a new possessiveness, with a kiss that said he wanted — needed — loved her.

Closing her eyes, her confusion dying away, Roberta gave herself up in delight to the kiss. It was hard to believe her dreams had come true, but here was the man she loved, saying all the things she'd longed to hear.

"I love you, Roberta," Justin whispered, and Roberta, her heart spinning wildly that at last she could say the words that had so long lived in her heart, murmured at once in reply, "Oh, Justin, I love you too!" And the next kiss was even sweeter than the one before, though not quite as perfect as the one that followed.

WITH SOMEBODY ELSE
Theresa Charles

Rosamond sets off for Cornwall with Hugo to meet his family, blissfully unaware of the shocks in store for her.

A SUMMER FOR STRANGERS
Claire Hamilton

Because she had lost her job, her flat and she had no money, Tabitha agreed to pose as Adam's future wife although she believed the scheme to be deceitful and cruel.

VILLA OF SINGING WATER
Angela Petron

The disquieting incidents that occurred at the Vatican and the Colosseum did not trouble Jan at first, but then they became increasingly unpleasant and alarming.

DOCTOR NAPIER'S NURSE
Pauline Ash

When cousins Midge and Derry are entered as probationer nurses on the same day but at different hospitals they agree to exchange identities.

A GIRL LIKE JULIE
Louise Ellis

Caroline absolutely adored Hugh Barrington, but then Julie Crane came into their lives. Julie was the kind of girl who attracts men without even trying.

COUNTRY DOCTOR
Paula Lindsay

When Evan Richmond bought a practice in a remote country village he did not realise that a casual encounter would lead to the loss of his heart.

ENCORE
Helga Moray

Craig and Janet realise that their true happiness lies with each other, but it is only under traumatic circumstances that they can be reunited.

NICOLETTE
Ivy Preston

When Grant Alston came back into her life, Nicolette was faced with a dilemma. Should she follow the path of duty or the path of love?

THE GOLDEN PUMA
Margaret Way

Catherine's time was spent looking after her father's Queensland farm. But what life was there without David, who wasn't interested in her?

HOSPITAL BY THE LAKE
Anne Durham

Nurse Marguerite Ingleby was always ready to become personally involved with her patients, to the despair of Brian Field, the Senior Surgical Registrar, who loved her.

VALLEY OF CONFLICT
David Farrell

Isolated in a hostel in the French Alps, Ann Russell sees her fiancé being seduced by a young girl. Then comes the avalanche that imperils their lives.

NURSE'S CHOICE
Peggy Gaddis

A proposal of marriage from the incredibly handsome and wealthy Reagan was enough to upset any girl — and Brooke Martin was no exception.

A DANGEROUS MAN
Anne Goring

Photographer Polly Burton was on safari in Mombasa when she met enigmatic Leon Hammond. But unpredictability was the name of the game where Leon was concerned.

PRECIOUS INHERITANCE
Joan Moules

Karen's new life working for an authoress took her from Sussex to a foreign airstrip and a kidnapping; to a real life adventure as gripping as any in the books she typed.

VISION OF LOVE
Grace Richmond

When Kathy takes over the rundown country kennels she finds Alec Stinton, a local vet, very helpful. But their friendship arouses bitter jealousy and a tragedy seems inevitable.

CRUSADING NURSE
Jane Converse

It was handsome Dr. Corbett who opened Nurse Susan Leighton's eyes and who set her off on a lonely crusade against some powerful enemies and a shattering struggle against the man she loved.

WILD ENCHANTMENT
Christina Green

Rowan's agreeable new boss had a dream of creating a famous perfume using her precious Silverstar, but Rowan's plans were very different.

DESERT ROMANCE
Irene Ord

Sally agrees to take her sister Pam's place as La Chartreuse the dancer, but she finds out there is more to it than dyeing her hair red and looking like her sister.

HEART OF ICE
Marie Sidney

How was January to know that not only would the warmth of the Swiss people thaw out her frozen heart, but that she too would play her part in helping someone to live again?

LUCKY IN LOVE
Margaret Wood

Companion-secretary to wealthy gambler Laura Duxford, who lived in Monaco, seemed to Melanie a fabulous job. Especially as Melanie had already lost her heart to Laura's son, Julian.

NURSE TO PRINCESS JASMINE
Lilian Woodward

Nick's surgeon brother, Tom, performs an operation on an Arabian princess, and she invites Tom, Nick and his fiancé to Omander, where a web of deceit and intrigue closes about them.

THE WAYWARD HEART
Eileen Barry

Disaster-prone Katherine's nickname was "Kate Calamity", but her boss went too far with an outrageous proposal, which because of her latest disaster, she could not refuse.

FOUR WEEKS IN WINTER
Jane Donnelly

Tessa wasn't looking forward to meeting Paul Mellor again — she had made a fool of herself over him once before. But was Orme Jared's solution to her problem likely to be the right one?

SURGERY BY THE SEA
Sheila Douglas

Medical student Meg hadn't really wanted to go and work with a G.P. on the Welsh coast although the job had its compensations. But Owen Roberts was certainly not one of them!

HEAVEN IS HIGH
Anne Hampson

The new heir to the Manor of Marbeck had been found. But it was rather unfortunate that when he arrived unexpectedly he found an uninvited guest, complete with stetson and high boots.

LOVE WILL COME
Sarah Devon

June Baker's boss was not really her idea of her ideal man, but when she went from third typist to boss's secretary overnight she began to change her mind.

ESCAPE TO ROMANCE
Kay Winchester

Oliver and Jean first met on Swale Island. They were both trying to begin their lives afresh, but neither had bargained for complications from the past.

CASTLE IN THE SUN
Cora Mayne

Emma's invalid sister, Kym, needed a warm climate, and Emma jumped at the chance of a job on a Mediterranean island. But Emma soon finds that intrigues and hazards lurk on the sunlit isle.

BEWARE OF LOVE
Kay Winchester

Carol Brampton resumes her nursing career when her family is killed in a car accident. With Dr. Patrick Farrell she begins to pick up the pieces of her life, but is bitterly hurt when insinuations are made about her to Patrick.

DARLING REBEL
Sarah Devon

When Jason Farradale's secretary met with an accident, her glamorous stand-in was quite unable to deal with one problem in particular.

THE PRICE OF PARADISE
Jane Arbor

It was a shock to Fern to meet her estranged husband on an island in the middle of the Indian Ocean, but to discover that her father had engineered it puzzled Fern. What did he hope to achieve?

DOCTOR IN PLASTER
Lisa Cooper

When Dr. Scott Sutcliffe is injured, Nurse Caroline Hurst has to cope with a very demanding private case. But when she realises her exasperating patient has stolen her heart, how can Caroline possibly stay?

A TOUCH OF HONEY
Lucy Gillen

Before she took the job as secretary to author Robert Dean, Cadie had heard how charming he was, but that wasn't her first impression at all.

ROMANTIC LEGACY
Cora Mayne

As kennelmaid to the Armstrongs, Ann Brown, had no idea that she would become the central figure in a web of mystery and intrigue.

THE RELENTLESS TIDE
Jill Murray

Steve Palmer shared Nurse Marie Blane's love of the sea and small boats. Marie's other passion was her step-brother. But when danger threatened who should she turn to — her step-brother or the man who stirred emotions in her heart?

ROMANCE IN NORWAY
Cora Mayne

Nancy Crawford hopes that her visit to Norway will help her to start life again. She certainly finds many surprises there, including unexpected happiness.

UNLOCK MY HEART
Honor Vincent

When Ruth Linton, a young widow with three children, inherits a house in the country, it seems to be the answer to her dreams. But Ruth's problems were only just beginning . . .

SWEET PROMISE
Janet Dailey

Erica had met Rafael in Mexico, where their relationship had been brief but dramatic. Now, over a year later in Texas, she had met him again — and he had the power to wreck her life.

SAFARI ENCOUNTER
Rosemary Carter

Jenny had to accept that she couldn't run her father's game park alone; so she let forceful Joshua Adams virtually take over. But Joshua took over her heart as well!